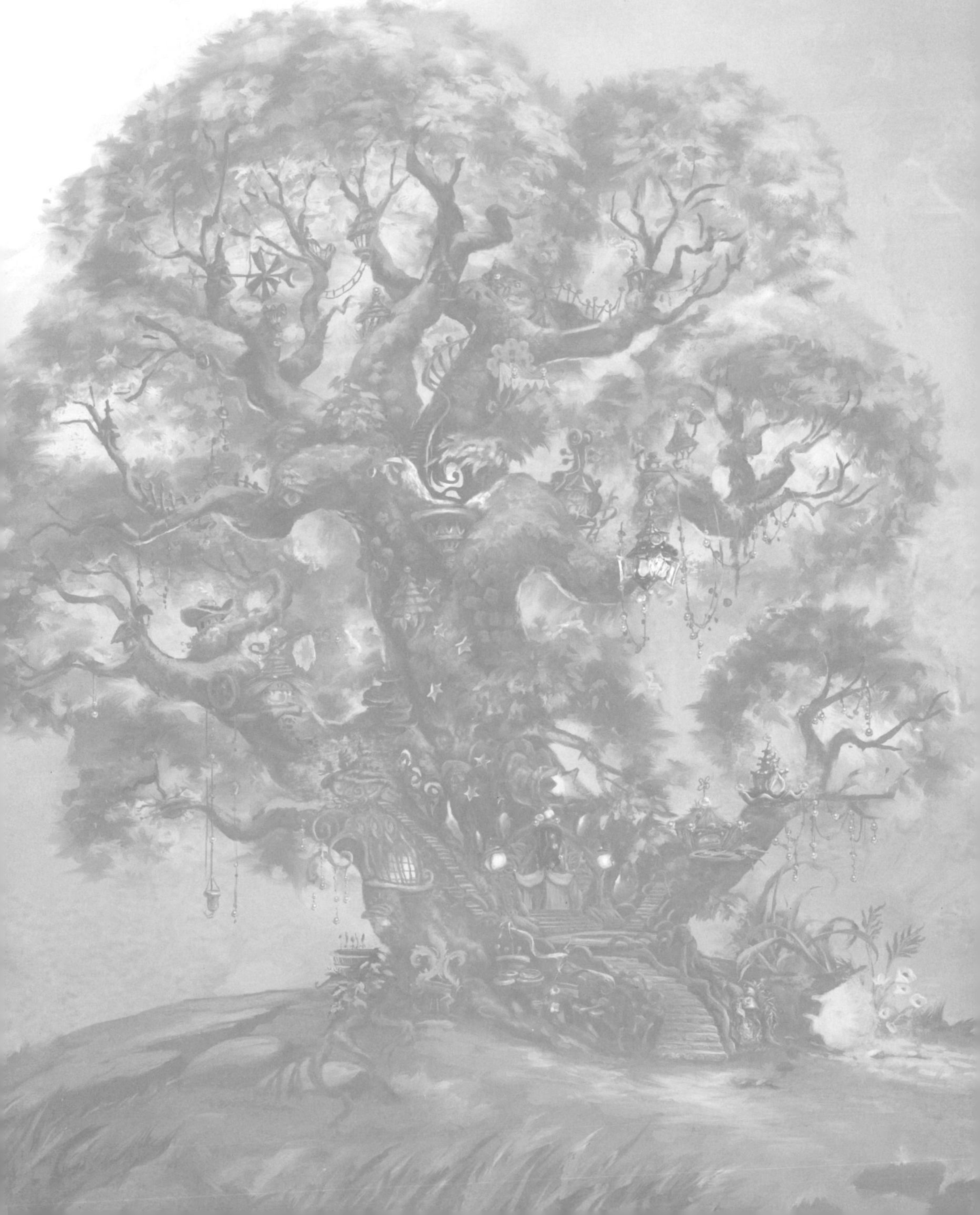

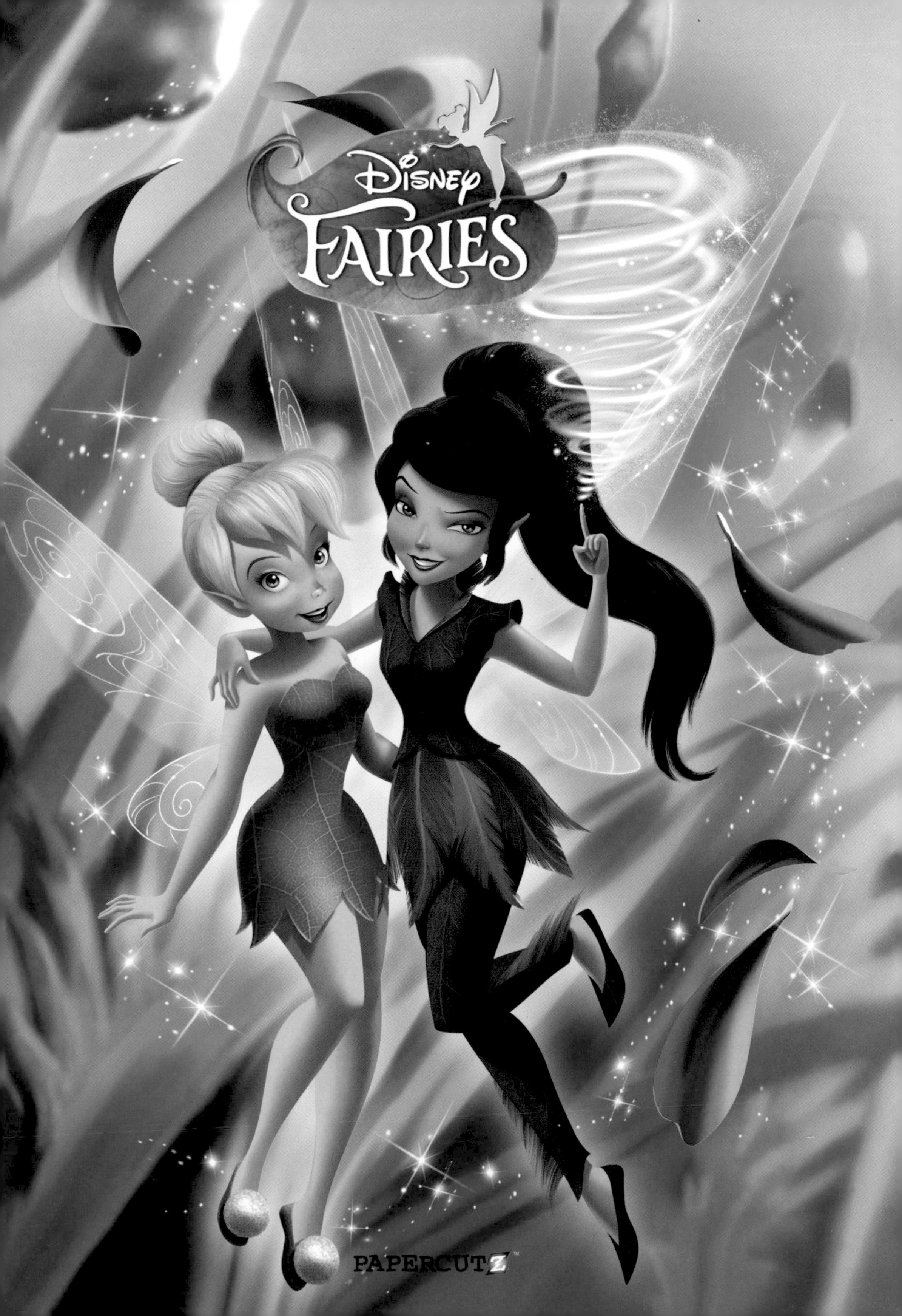
Disney
FAIRIES
PAPERCUTZ

DISNEY FAIRIES

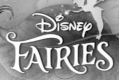

Graphic Novels Available from PAPERCUTZ

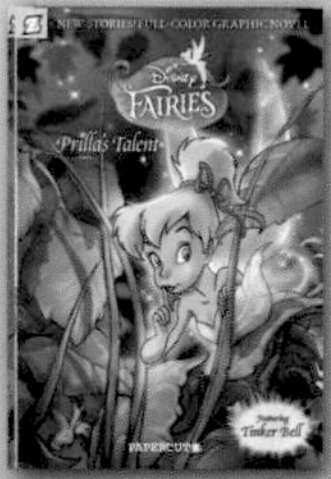

Graphic Novel #1
"Prilla's Talent"

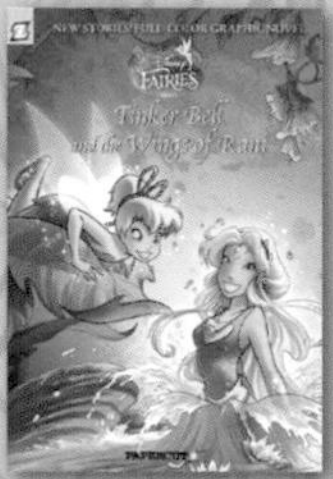

Graphic Novel #2
"Tinker Bell and the Wings of Rani"

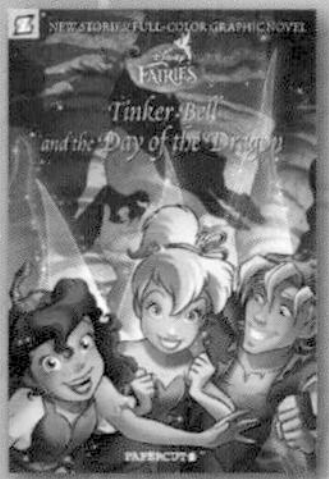

Graphic Novel #3
"Tinker Bell and the Day of the Dragon"

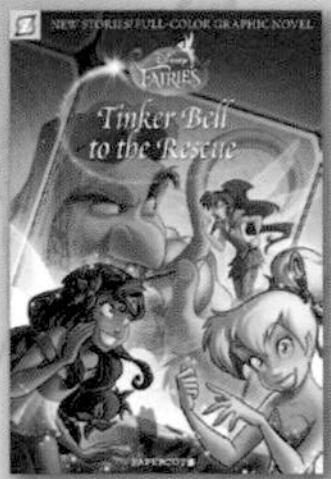

Graphic Novel #4
"Tinker Bell to the Rescue'

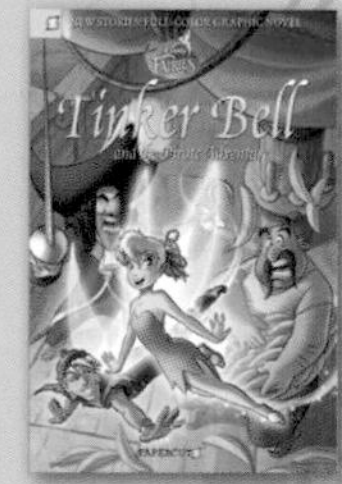

Graphic Novel #5
"Tinker Bell and the Pirate Adventure"

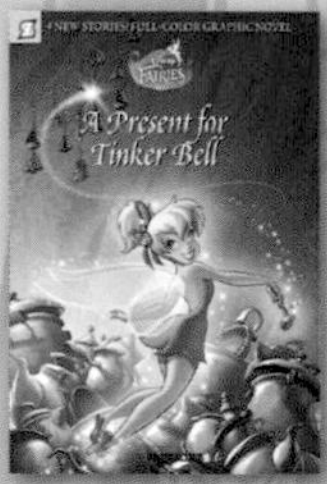

Graphic Novel #6
"A Present for Tinker Bell"

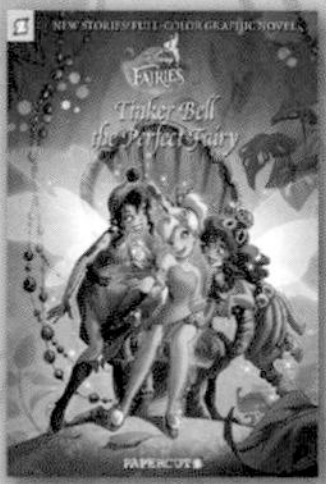

Graphic Novel #7
"Tinker Bell the Perfect Fairy"

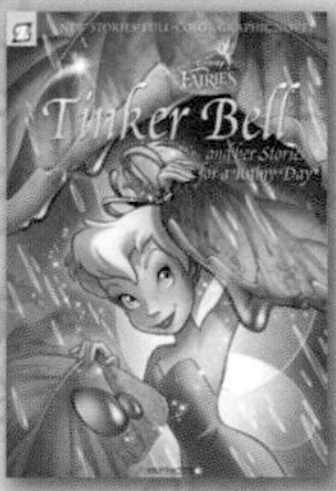

Graphic Novel #8
"Tinker Bell and her Storie for a Rainy Day"

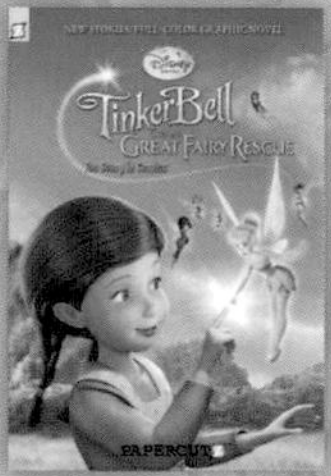

Tinker Bell and the Great Fairy Rescue

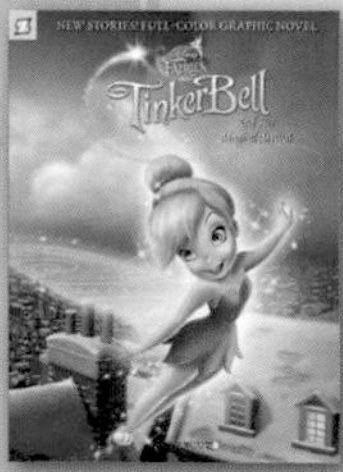

Graphic Novel #9
"Tinker Bell and her Magical Arrival"

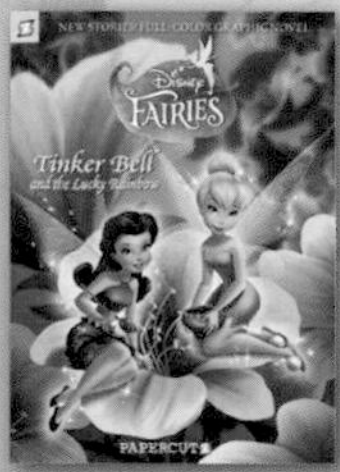

Graphic Novel #10
"Tinker Bell and the Lucky Rainbow"

Coming Soon:

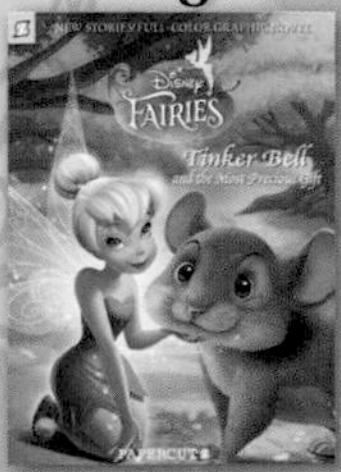

Graphic Novel #11
"Tinker Bell and the Most Precious Gift"

DISNEY FAIRIES graphic novels are available in paperback for $7.99 each; in hardcover for $12.99 each except #5, $6.99PB, $10.99HC. #6-11 are $7.99PB $11.99HC. Tinker Bell and the Great Fairy rescue is $9.99 in hardcover only Available at booksellers everywhere.

See more at www.papercutz.com

Or you can order from us: please add $4.00 for postage and handling for first book, and add $1.00 for each additional book. Please make check payable to NBM Publishing. Send to: Papercutz, 160 Broadway, Suite 700, East Wing, New York, NY 10038 or call 800 886 1223 (9-6 EST M-F) MC-Visa-Amex accepted.

DISNEY FAIRIES

#10 "Tinker Bell and the Lucky Rainbow"

Contents

PAPERCUTZ™

NEW YORK

"The Enchanted Gem"
Script: Carlo Panaro
Revised Dialogue: Cortney Faye Powell
and Jim Salicrup
Pencils: Antonello Dalena
Inks: Manuela Razzi
Color: Kawaii Creative Studio
Letters: Janice Chiang
Page 5 art:
Concept: Tea Orsi
Pencils and Inks: Sara Storino
Color: Andrea Cagol

"Tinker Bell and the Lucky Rainbow"
Concept and Script: Paola Mulazzi
Revised Dialogue: Cortney Faye Powell
and Jim Salicrup
Layout: Anna Merli
Pencils: Sara Storino
Inks: Marina Baggio
Color: Litomilano
Letters: Janice Chiang
Page 31 Art:
Concept: Tea Orsi
Pencils and Inks: Sara Storino
Color: Andrea Cagol

"A Winter Fairy Concert"
Concept and Script: Augusto Macchetto
Revised Dialogue: Cortney Faye Powell
and Jim Salicrup
Layout: Anna Merli
Pencils: Sara Storino
Inks: Marina Baggio
Color: Litomilano
Letters: Janice Chiang
Page 18 Art:
Concept: Tea Orsi
Pencils and Inks: Sara Storino
Color: Andrea Cagol

"The Vain Flower"
Script: Tea Orsi
Revised Dialogue: Cortney Faye Powell
and Jim Salicrup
Layout: Antonello Dalena
Pencils: Manuela Razzi
Inks: Marina Baggio
Color: Studio Kawaii
Letters: Janice Chiang
Page 44 Art:
Concept: Tea Orsi
Pencils and Inks: Sara Storino
Color: Andrea Cagol

Nelson Design Group, LLC – Production
Special Thanks – Shiho Tilley
Michael Petranek – Associate Editor
Jim Salicrup
Editor-in-Chief

ISBN: 978-1-59707-367-7 paperback edition

ISBN: 978-1-59707-368-4 hardcover edition

Printed in Singapore.
December 2012
by Tien Wah Press PTE LTD
4 Pandan Crescent
Singapore 128475

Distributed by Macmillan

First Papercutz Printing

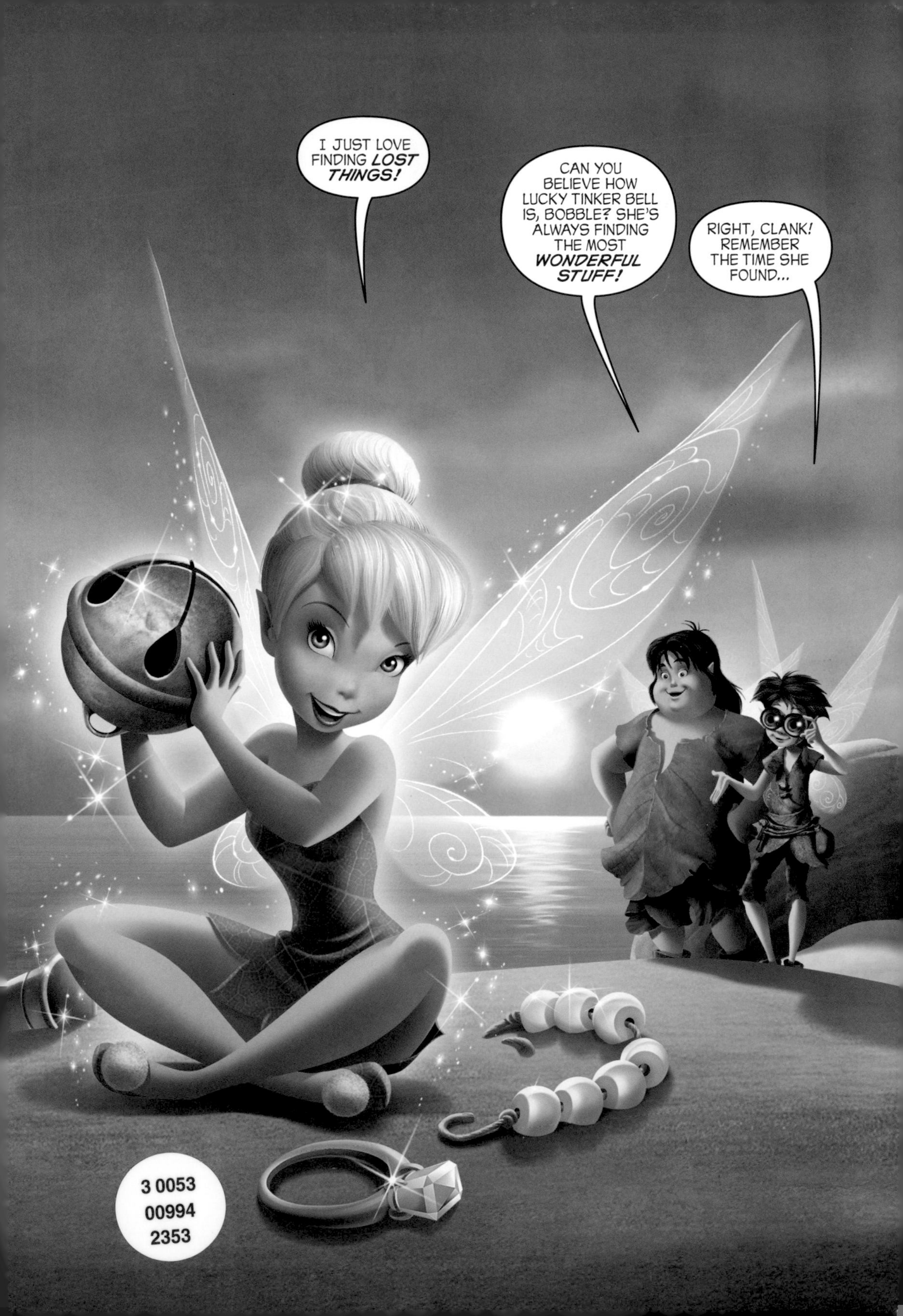
I JUST LOVE FINDING LOST THINGS!
CAN YOU BELIEVE HOW LUCKY TINKER BELL IS, BOBBLE? SHE'S ALWAYS FINDING THE MOST WONDERFUL STUFF!
RIGHT, CLANK! REMEMBER THE TIME SHE FOUND...

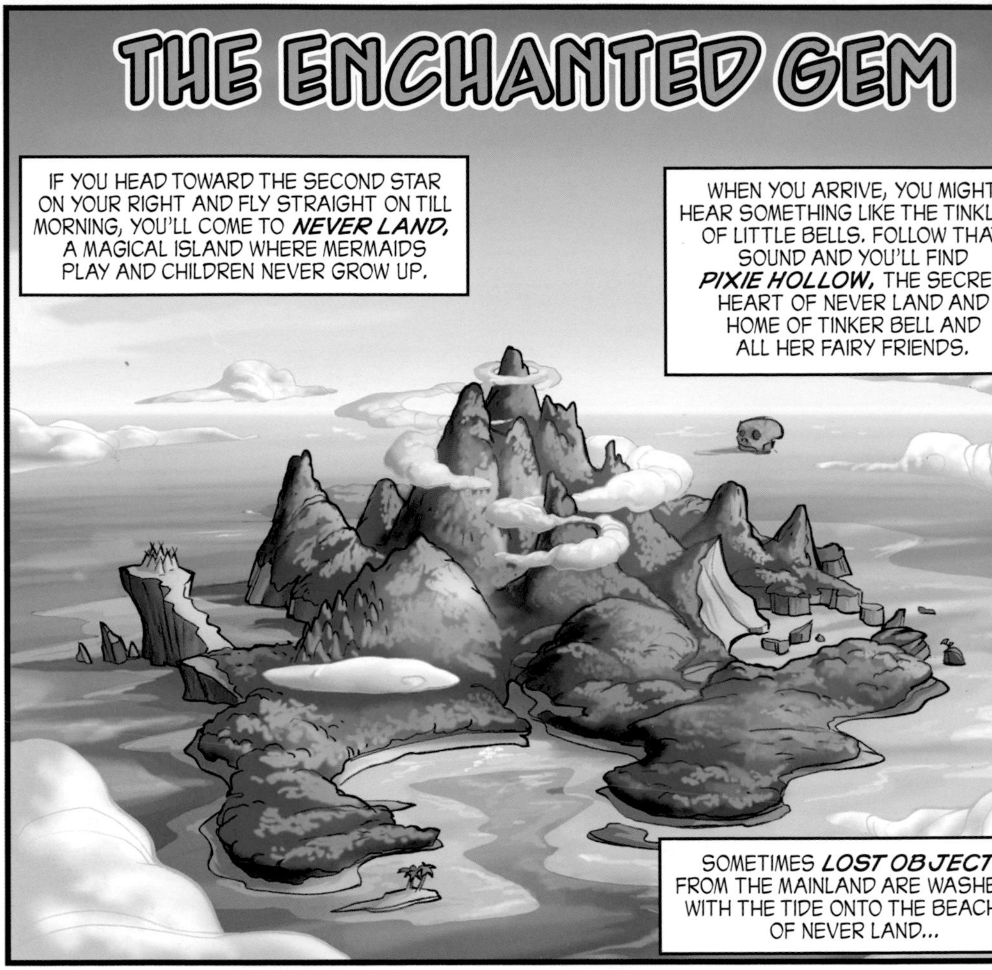
THE ENCHANTED GEM
IF YOU HEAD TOWARD THE SECOND STAR ON YOUR RIGHT AND FLY STRAIGHT ON TILL MORNING, YOU'LL COME TO NEVER LAND, A MAGICAL ISLAND WHERE MERMAIDS PLAY AND CHILDREN NEVER GROW UP.
WHEN YOU ARRIVE, YOU MIGHT HEAR SOMETHING LIKE THE TINKLING OF LITTLE BELLS. FOLLOW THAT SOUND AND YOU'LL FIND PIXIE HOLLOW, THE SECRET HEART OF NEVER LAND AND HOME OF TINKER BELL AND ALL HER FAIRY FRIENDS.
SOMETIMES LOST OBJECTS FROM THE MAINLAND ARE WASHED IN WITH THE TIDE ONTO THE BEACHES OF NEVER LAND...

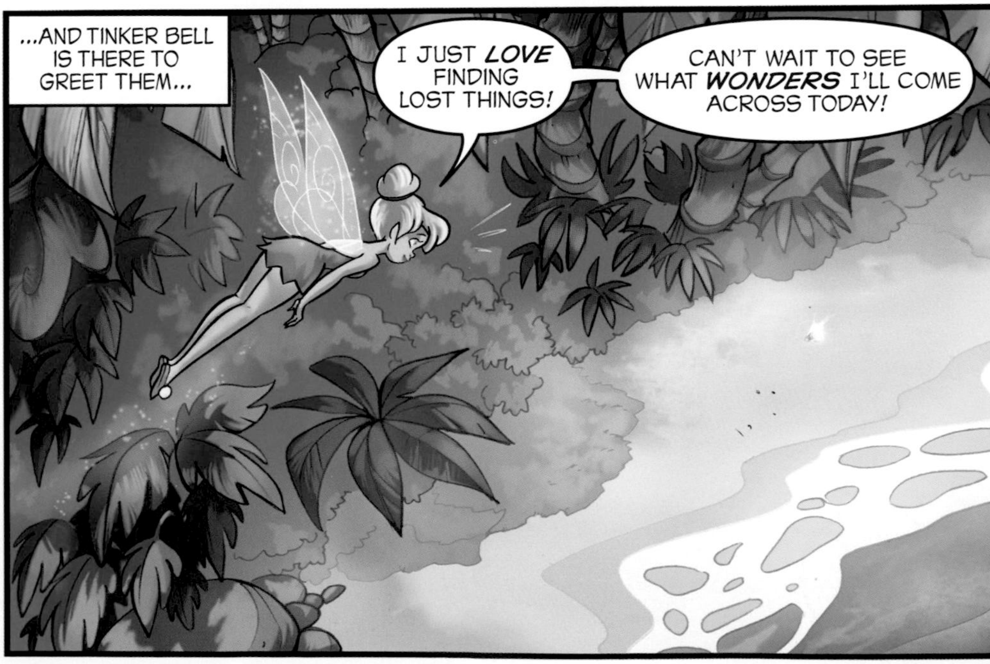
...AND TINKER BELL IS THERE TO GREET THEM...
I JUST LOVE FINDING LOST THINGS!
CAN'T WAIT TO SEE WHAT WONDERS I'LL COME ACROSS TODAY!

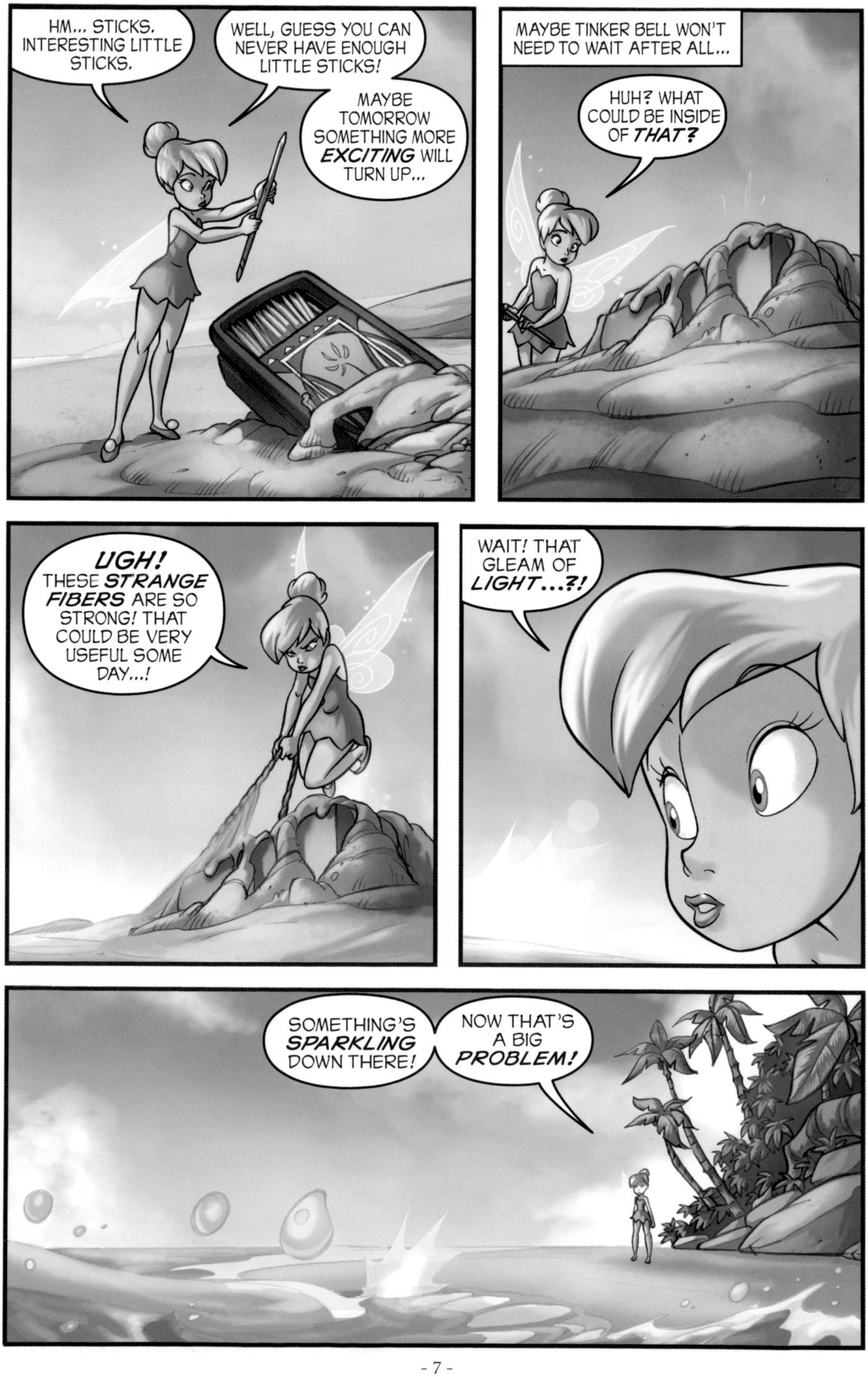
HM... STICKS. INTERESTING LITTLE STICKS.
WELL, GUESS YOU CAN NEVER HAVE ENOUGH LITTLE STICKS!
MAYBE TOMORROW SOMETHING MORE EXCITING WILL TURN UP...
MAYBE TINKER BELL WON'T NEED TO WAIT AFTER ALL...
HUH? WHAT COULD BE INSIDE OF THAT?
UGH! THESE STRANGE FIBERS ARE SO STRONG! THAT COULD BE VERY USEFUL SOME DAY...!
WAIT! THAT GLEAM OF LIGHT...?!
SOMETHING'S SPARKLING DOWN THERE!
NOW THAT'S A BIG PROBLEM!

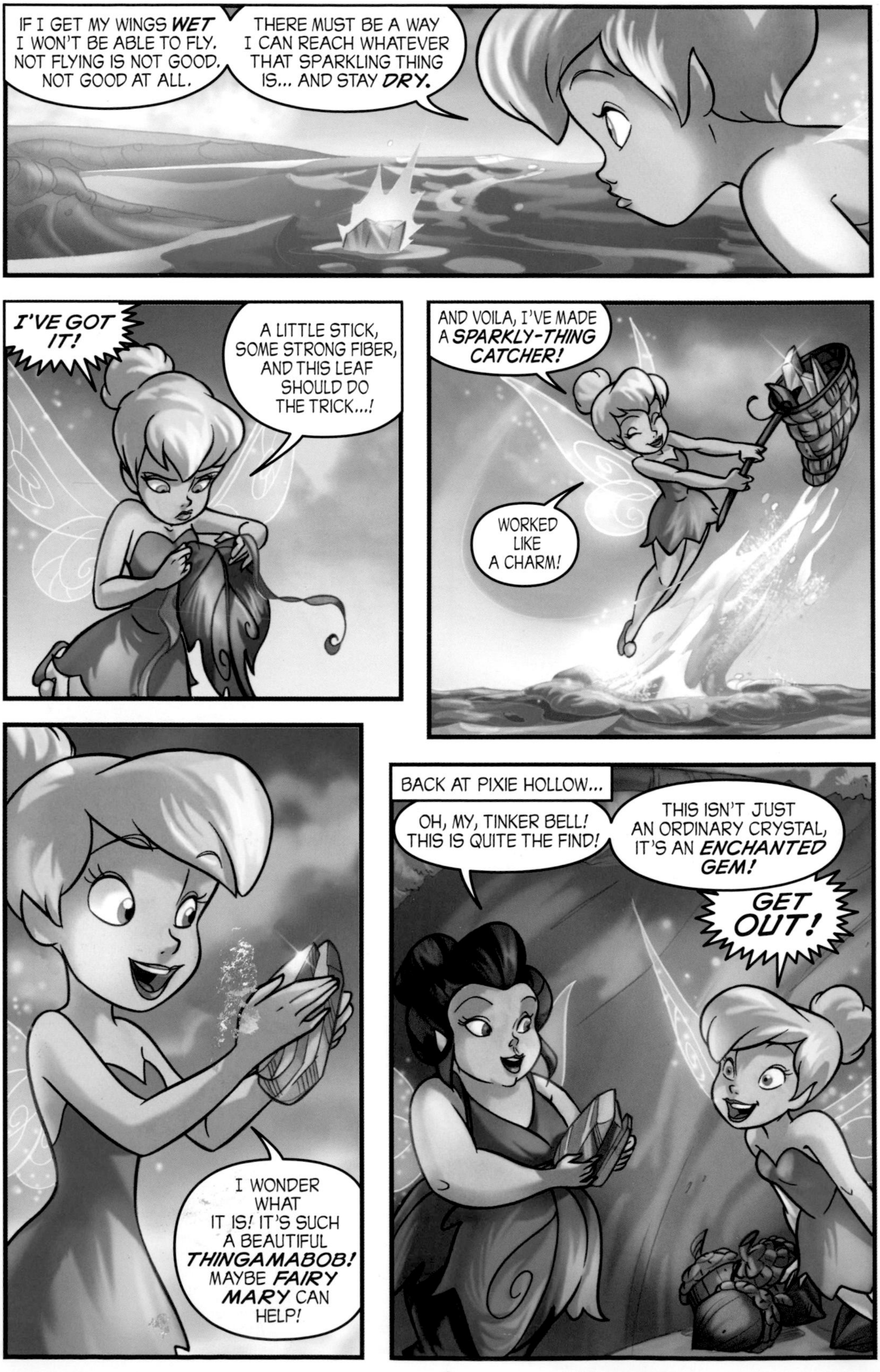
IF I GET MY WINGS WET I WON'T BE ABLE TO FLY. NOT FLYING IS NOT GOOD. NOT GOOD AT ALL.
THERE MUST BE A WAY I CAN REACH WHATEVER THAT SPARKLING THING IS... AND STAY DRY.
I'VE GOT IT!
A LITTLE STICK, SOME STRONG FIBER, AND THIS LEAF SHOULD DO THE TRICK...!
AND VOILA, I'VE MADE A SPARKLY-THING CATCHER!
WORKED LIKE A CHARM!
I WONDER WHAT IT IS! IT'S SUCH A BEAUTIFUL THINGAMABOB! MAYBE FAIRY MARY CAN HELP!
BACK AT PIXIE HOLLOW...
OH, MY, TINKER BELL! THIS IS QUITE THE FIND!
THIS ISN'T JUST AN ORDINARY CRYSTAL, IT'S AN ENCHANTED GEM!
GET OUT!

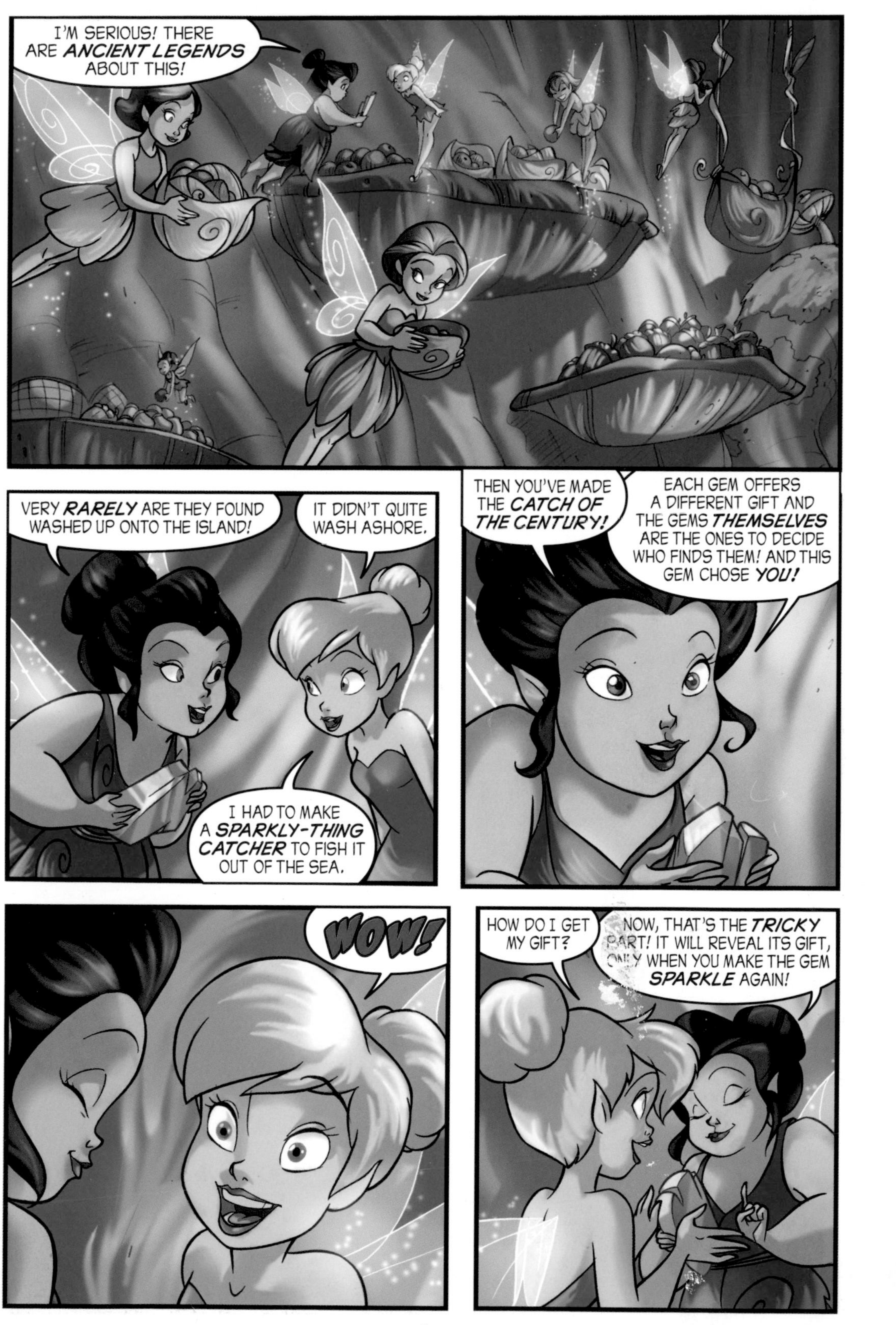
I'M SERIOUS! THERE ARE ANCIENT LEGENDS ABOUT THIS!
VERY RARELY ARE THEY FOUND WASHED UP ONTO THE ISLAND!
IT DIDN'T QUITE WASH ASHORE.
I HAD TO MAKE A SPARKLY-THING CATCHER TO FISH IT OUT OF THE SEA.
THEN YOU'VE MADE THE CATCH OF THE CENTURY!
EACH GEM OFFERS A DIFFERENT GIFT AND THE GEMS THEMSELVES ARE THE ONES TO DECIDE WHO FINDS THEM! AND THIS GEM CHOSE YOU!
WOW!
HOW DO I GET MY GIFT?
NOW, THAT'S THE TRICKY PART! IT WILL REVEAL ITS GIFT, ONLY WHEN YOU MAKE THE GEM SPARKLE AGAIN!

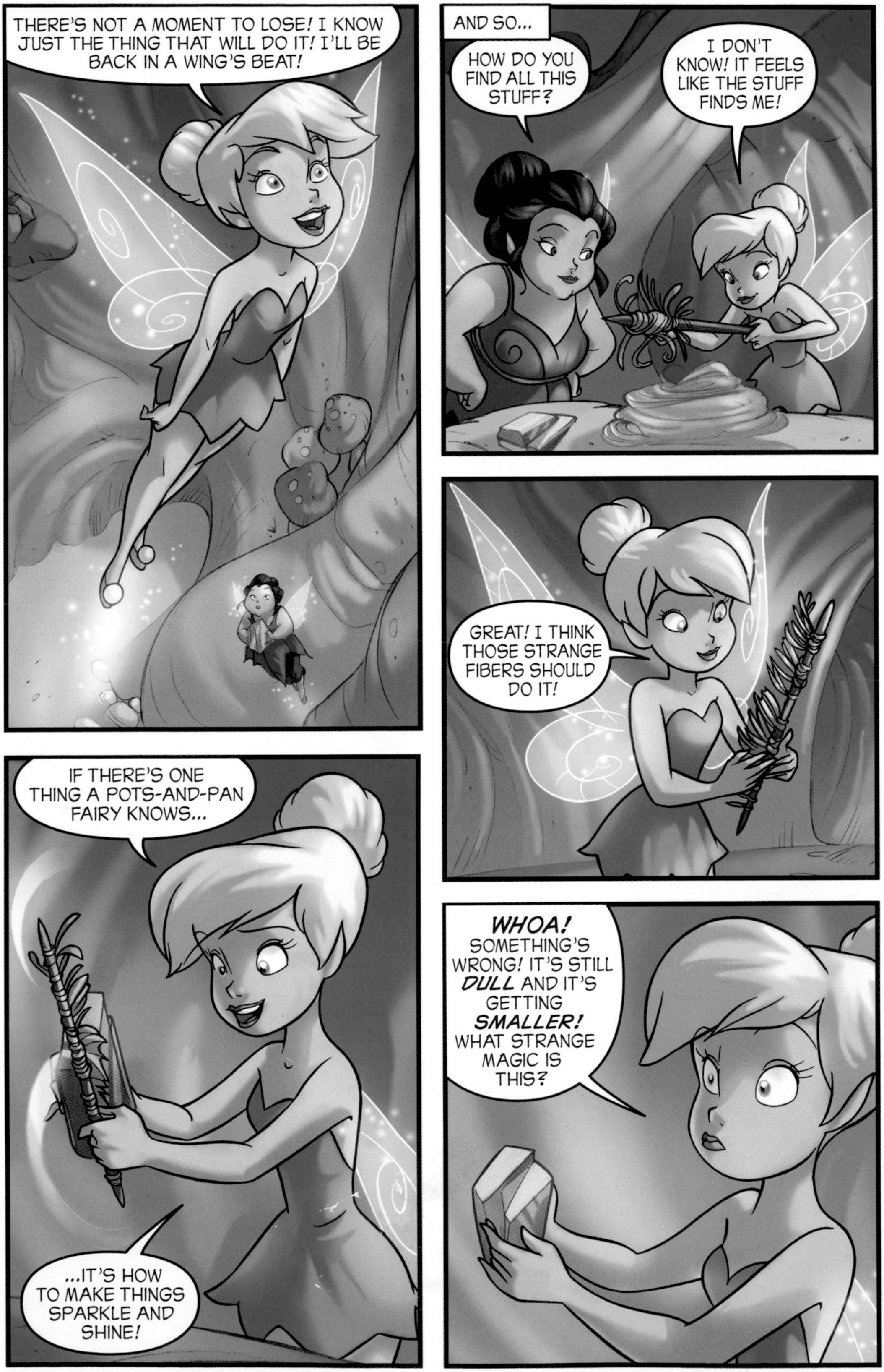
THERE'S NOT A MOMENT TO LOSE! I KNOW JUST THE THING THAT WILL DO IT! I'LL BE BACK IN A WING'S BEAT!
AND SO...
HOW DO YOU FIND ALL THIS STUFF?
I DON'T KNOW! IT FEELS LIKE THE STUFF FINDS ME!
IF THERE'S ONE THING A POTS-AND-PAN FAIRY KNOWS...
...IT'S HOW TO MAKE THINGS SPARKLE AND SHINE!
GREAT! I THINK THOSE STRANGE FIBERS SHOULD DO IT!
WHOA! SOMETHING'S WRONG! IT'S STILL DULL AND IT'S GETTING SMALLER! WHAT STRANGE MAGIC IS THIS?

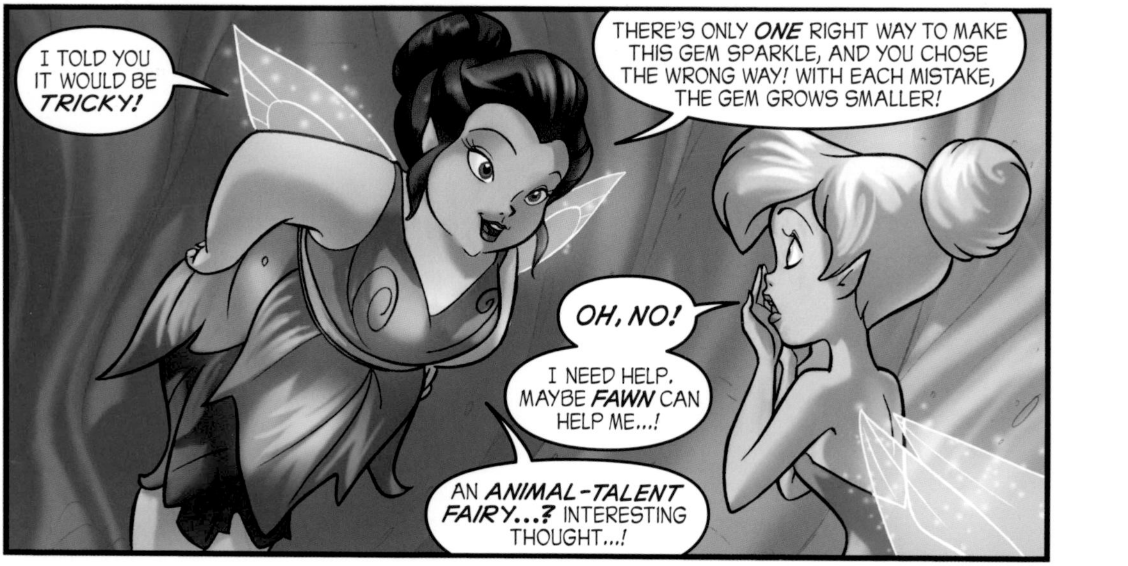
I TOLD YOU IT WOULD BE *TRICKY!*
THERE'S ONLY *ONE* RIGHT WAY TO MAKE THIS GEM SPARKLE, AND YOU CHOSE THE WRONG WAY! WITH EACH MISTAKE, THE GEM GROWS SMALLER!
OH, NO!
I NEED HELP. MAYBE *FAWN* CAN HELP ME...!
AN *ANIMAL-TALENT FAIRY...?* INTERESTING THOUGHT...!

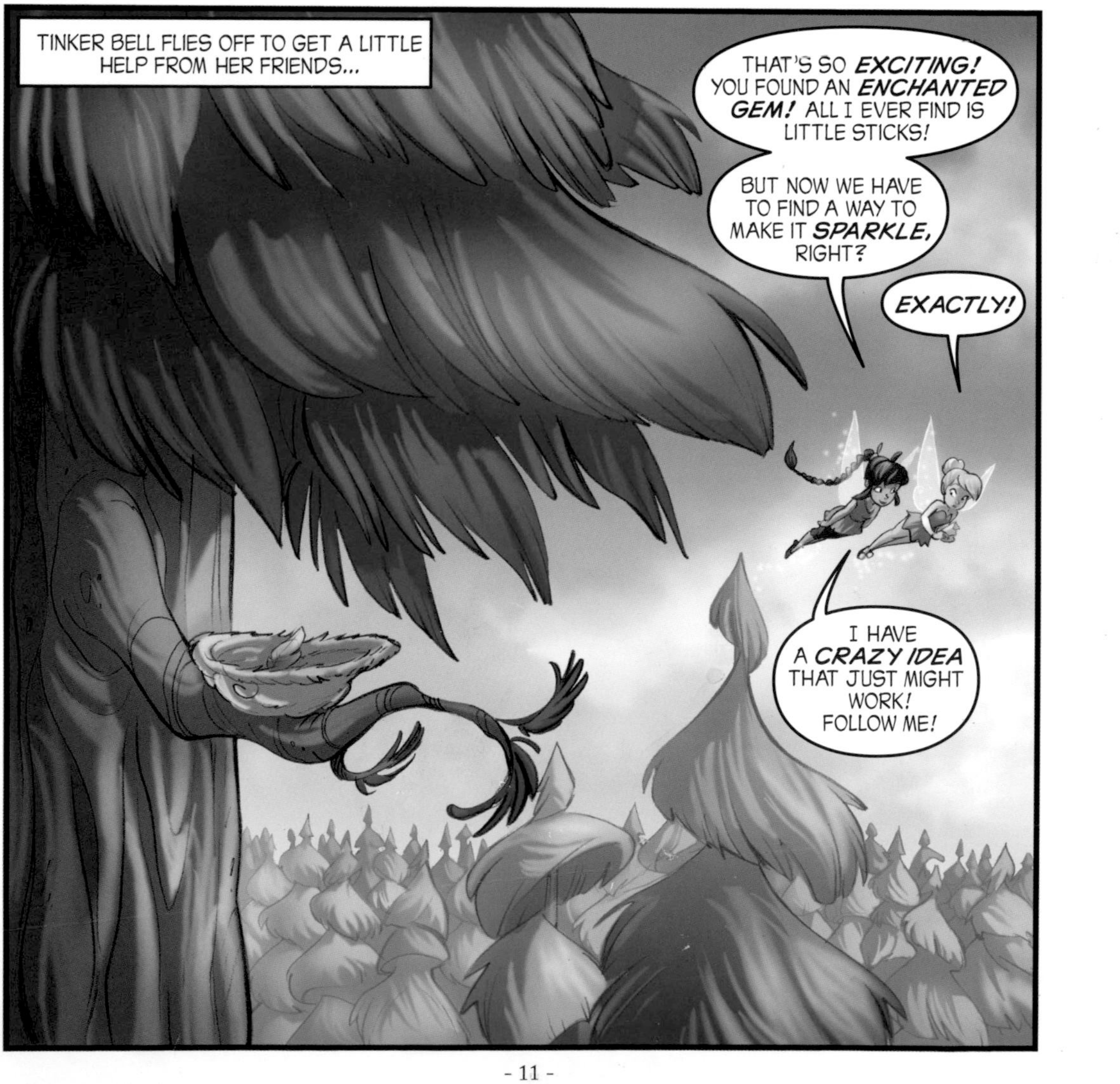
TINKER BELL FLIES OFF TO GET A LITTLE HELP FROM HER FRIENDS...
THAT'S SO *EXCITING!* YOU FOUND AN *ENCHANTED GEM!* ALL I EVER FIND IS LITTLE STICKS!
BUT NOW WE HAVE TO FIND A WAY TO MAKE IT *SPARKLE,* RIGHT?
EXACTLY!
I HAVE A *CRAZY IDEA* THAT JUST MIGHT WORK! FOLLOW ME!

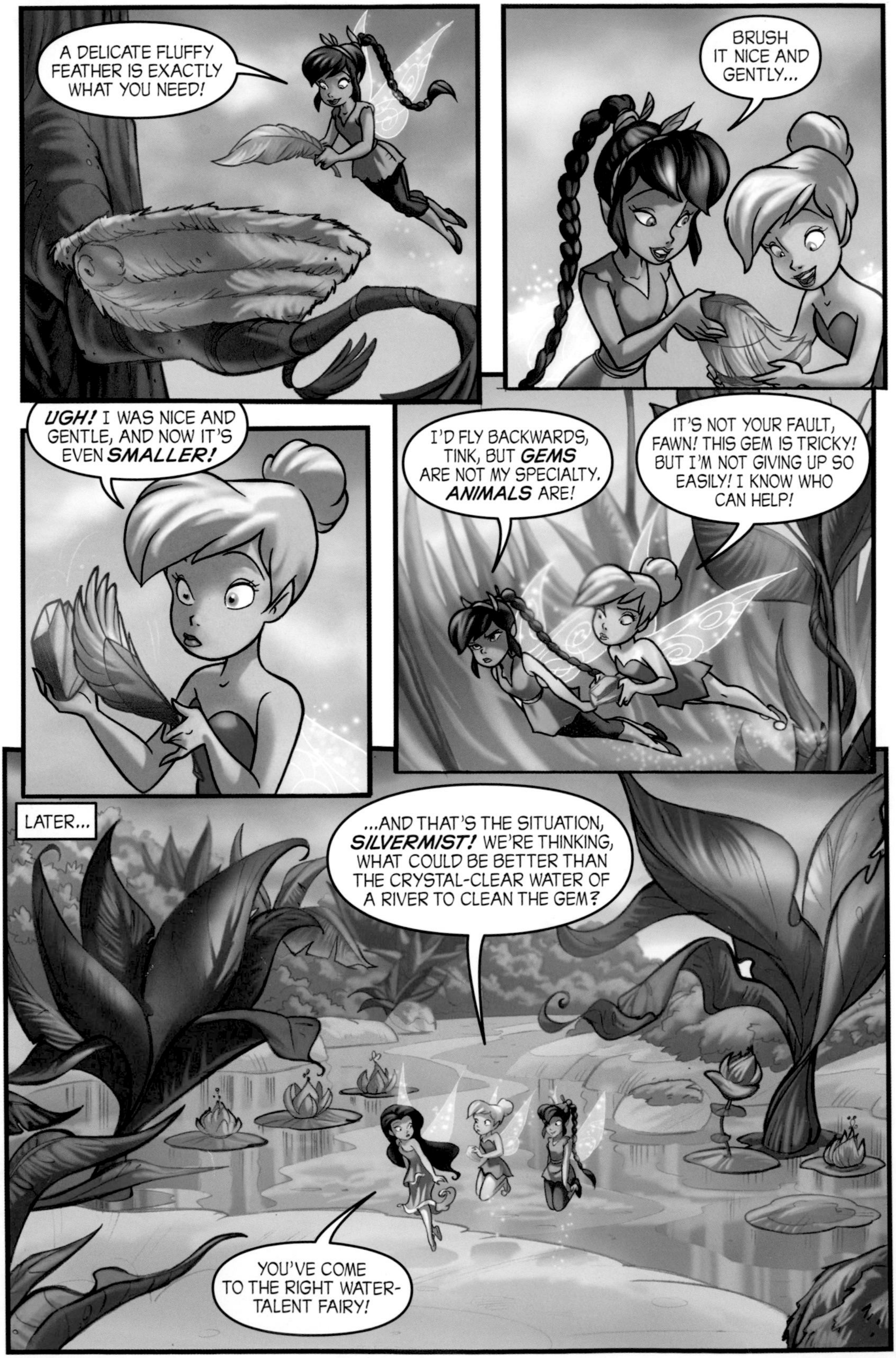
A DELICATE FLUFFY FEATHER IS EXACTLY WHAT YOU NEED!
BRUSH IT NICE AND GENTLY...
UGH! I WAS NICE AND GENTLE, AND NOW IT'S EVEN SMALLER!
I'D FLY BACKWARDS, TINK, BUT GEMS ARE NOT MY SPECIALTY. ANIMALS ARE!
IT'S NOT YOUR FAULT, FAWN! THIS GEM IS TRICKY! BUT I'M NOT GIVING UP SO EASILY! I KNOW WHO CAN HELP!
LATER...
...AND THAT'S THE SITUATION, SILVERMIST! WE'RE THINKING, WHAT COULD BE BETTER THAN THE CRYSTAL-CLEAR WATER OF A RIVER TO CLEAN THE GEM?
YOU'VE COME TO THE RIGHT WATER-TALENT FAIRY!

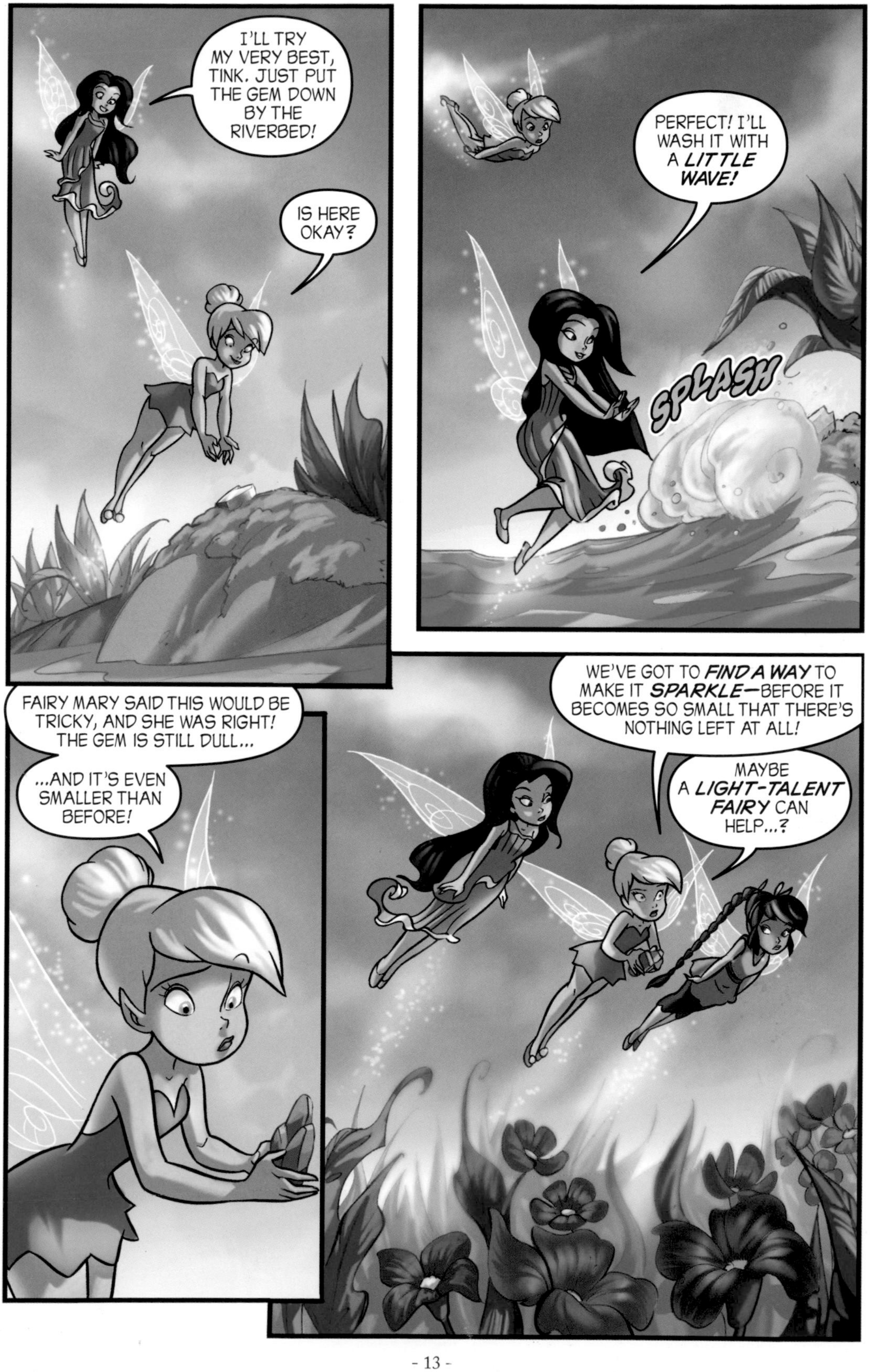
I'LL TRY MY VERY BEST, TINK. JUST PUT THE GEM DOWN BY THE RIVERBED!
IS HERE OKAY?
PERFECT! I'LL WASH IT WITH A LITTLE WAVE!
SPLASH
FAIRY MARY SAID THIS WOULD BE TRICKY, AND SHE WAS RIGHT! THE GEM IS STILL DULL...
...AND IT'S EVEN SMALLER THAN BEFORE!
WE'VE GOT TO FIND A WAY TO MAKE IT SPARKLE—BEFORE IT BECOMES SO SMALL THAT THERE'S NOTHING LEFT AT ALL!
MAYBE A LIGHT-TALENT FAIRY CAN HELP...?

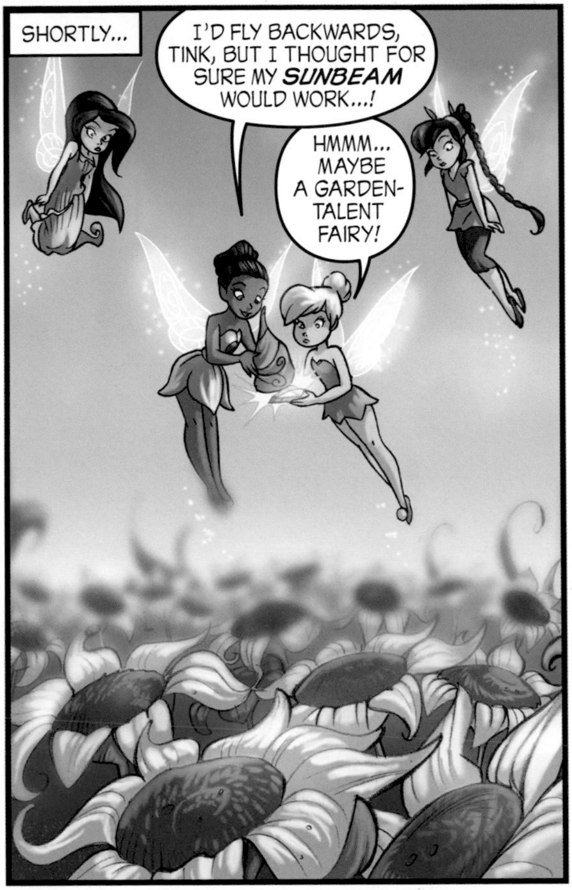
SHORTLY...
I'D FLY BACKWARDS, TINK, BUT I THOUGHT FOR SURE MY SUNBEAM WOULD WORK...!
HMMM... MAYBE A GARDEN-TALENT FAIRY!

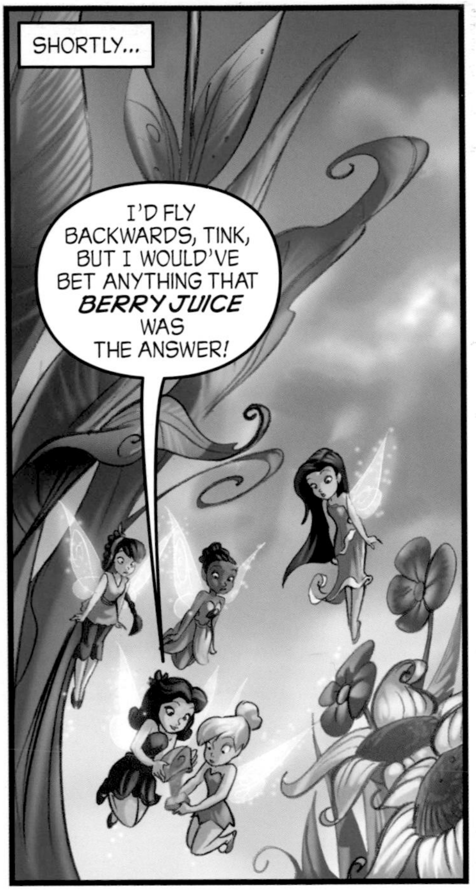
SHORTLY...
I'D FLY BACKWARDS, TINK, BUT I WOULD'VE BET ANYTHING THAT BERRY JUICE WAS THE ANSWER!

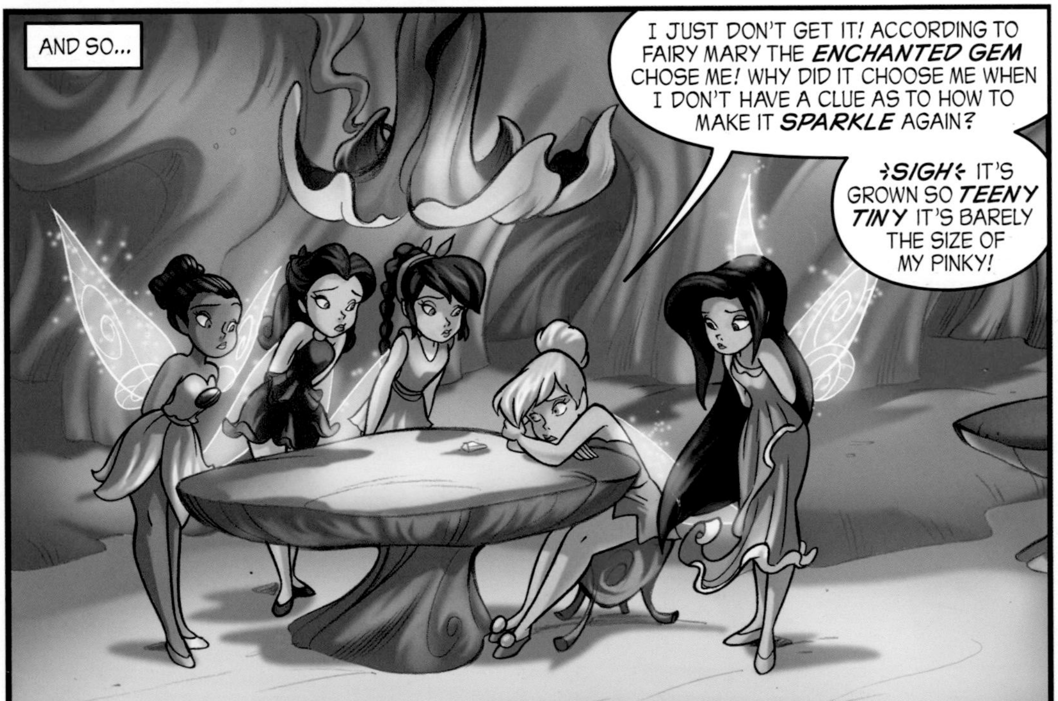
AND SO...
I JUST DON'T GET IT! ACCORDING TO FAIRY MARY THE ENCHANTED GEM CHOSE ME! WHY DID IT CHOOSE ME WHEN I DON'T HAVE A CLUE AS TO HOW TO MAKE IT SPARKLE AGAIN?
SIGH IT'S GROWN SO TEENY TINY IT'S BARELY THE SIZE OF MY PINKY!

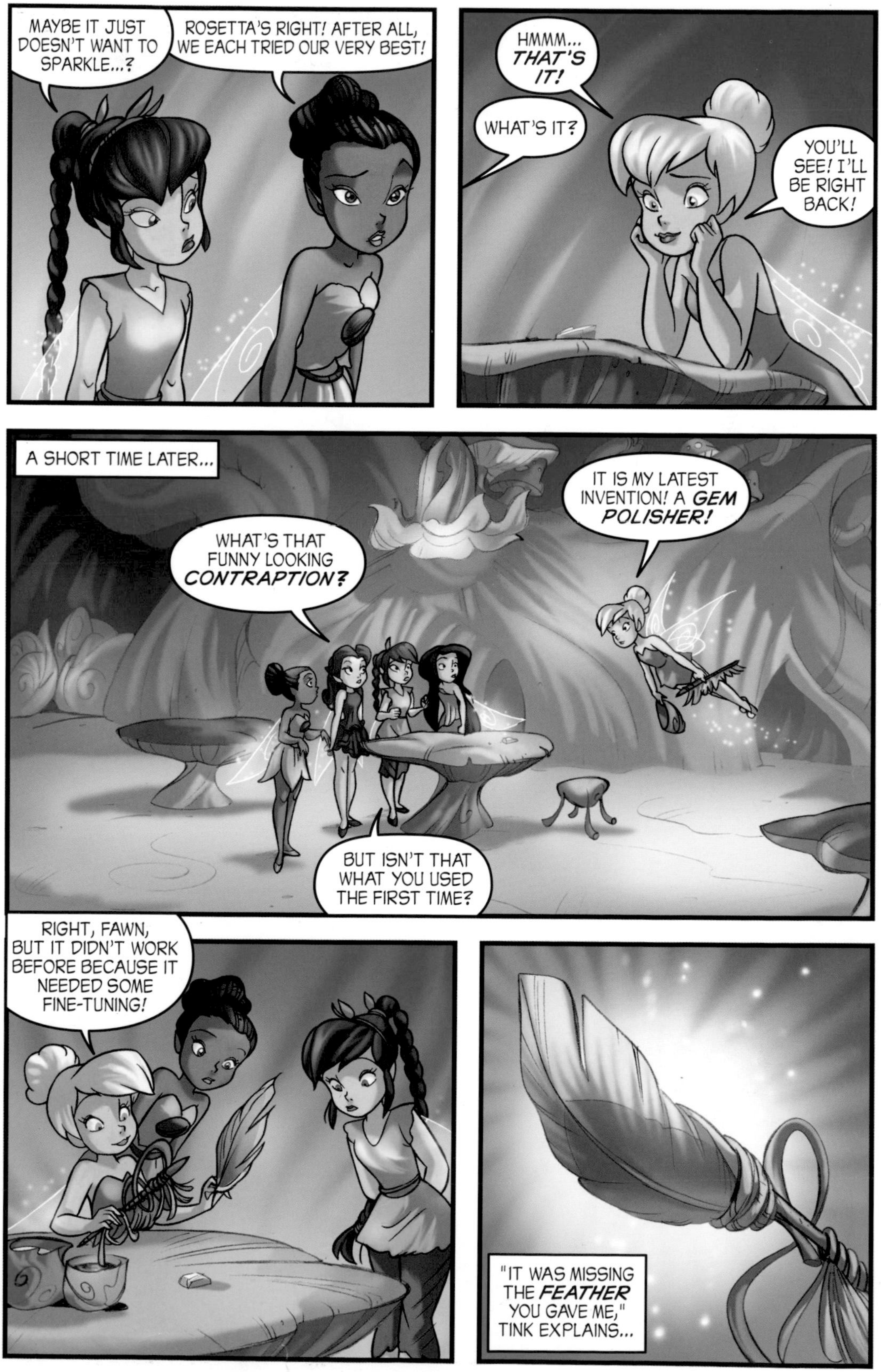
MAYBE IT JUST DOESN'T WANT TO SPARKLE...?
ROSETTA'S RIGHT! AFTER ALL, WE EACH TRIED OUR VERY BEST!
HMMM... THAT'S IT!
WHAT'S IT?
YOU'LL SEE! I'LL BE RIGHT BACK!
A SHORT TIME LATER...
WHAT'S THAT FUNNY LOOKING CONTRAPTION?
IT IS MY LATEST INVENTION! A GEM POLISHER!
BUT ISN'T THAT WHAT YOU USED THE FIRST TIME?
RIGHT, FAWN, BUT IT DIDN'T WORK BEFORE BECAUSE IT NEEDED SOME FINE-TUNING!
"IT WAS MISSING THE FEATHER YOU GAVE ME," TINK EXPLAINS...

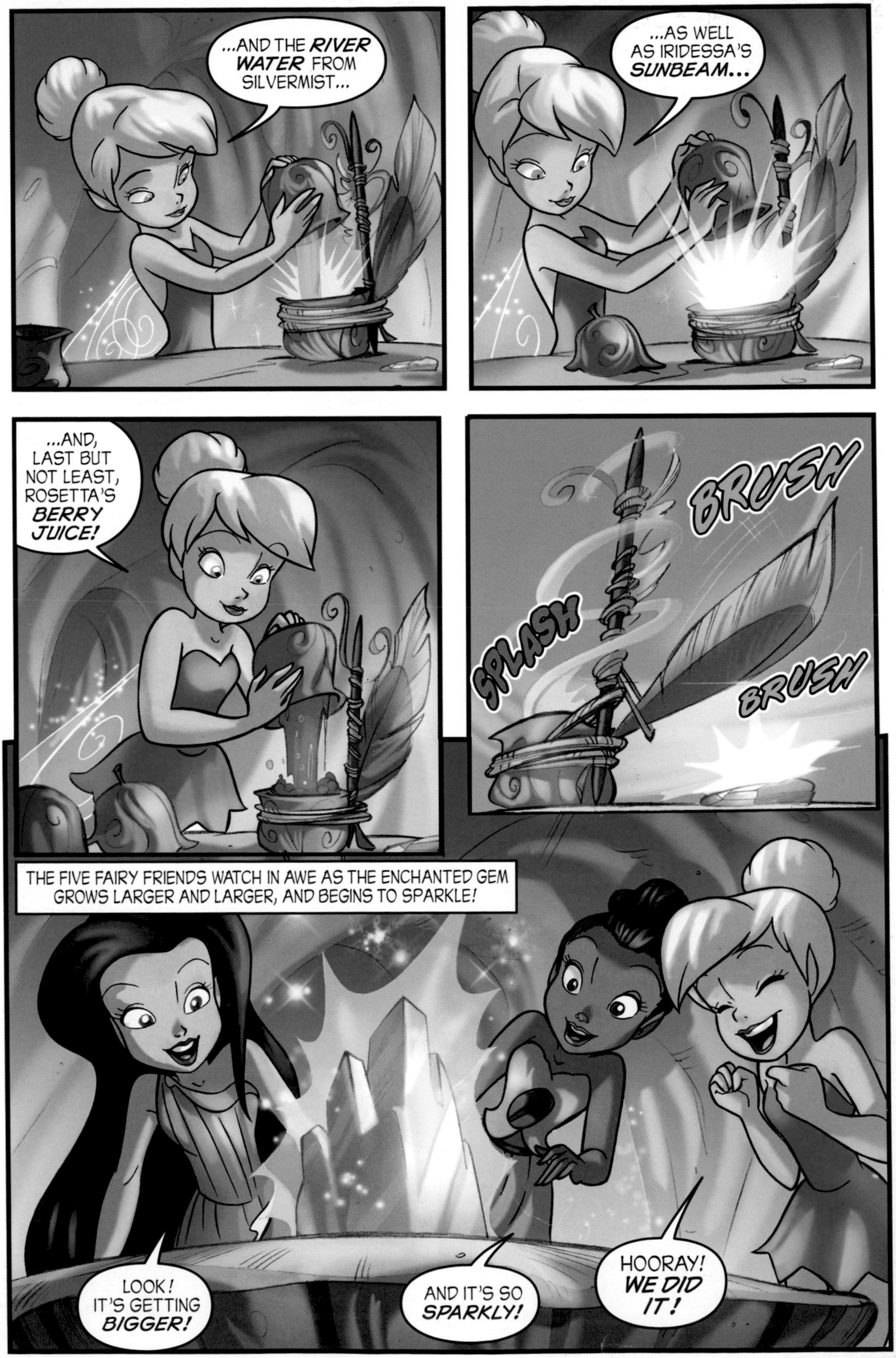
...AND THE RIVER WATER FROM SILVERMIST...
...AS WELL AS IRIDESSA'S SUNBEAM...
...AND, LAST BUT NOT LEAST, ROSETTA'S BERRY JUICE!
BRUSH
SPLASH
BRUSH
THE FIVE FAIRY FRIENDS WATCH IN AWE AS THE ENCHANTED GEM GROWS LARGER AND LARGER, AND BEGINS TO SPARKLE!
LOOK! IT'S GETTING BIGGER!
AND IT'S SO SPARKLY!
HOORAY! WE DID IT!

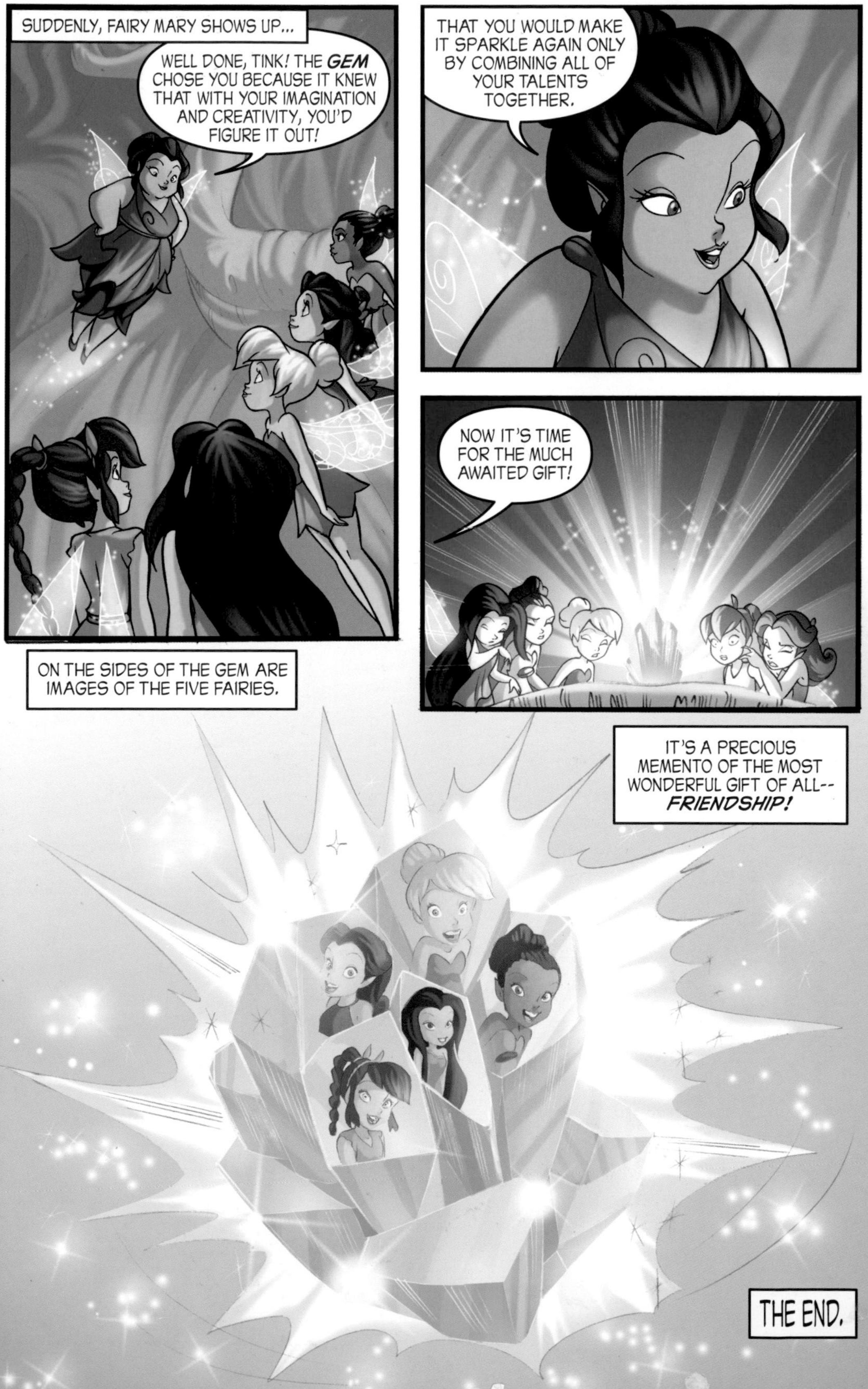
SUDDENLY, FAIRY MARY SHOWS UP...
WELL DONE, TINK! THE **GEM** CHOSE YOU BECAUSE IT KNEW THAT WITH YOUR IMAGINATION AND CREATIVITY, YOU'D FIGURE IT OUT!
THAT YOU WOULD MAKE IT SPARKLE AGAIN ONLY BY COMBINING ALL OF YOUR TALENTS TOGETHER.
NOW IT'S TIME FOR THE MUCH AWAITED GIFT!
ON THE SIDES OF THE GEM ARE IMAGES OF THE FIVE FAIRIES.
IT'S A PRECIOUS MEMENTO OF THE MOST WONDERFUL GIFT OF ALL-- **FRIENDSHIP!**
THE END.

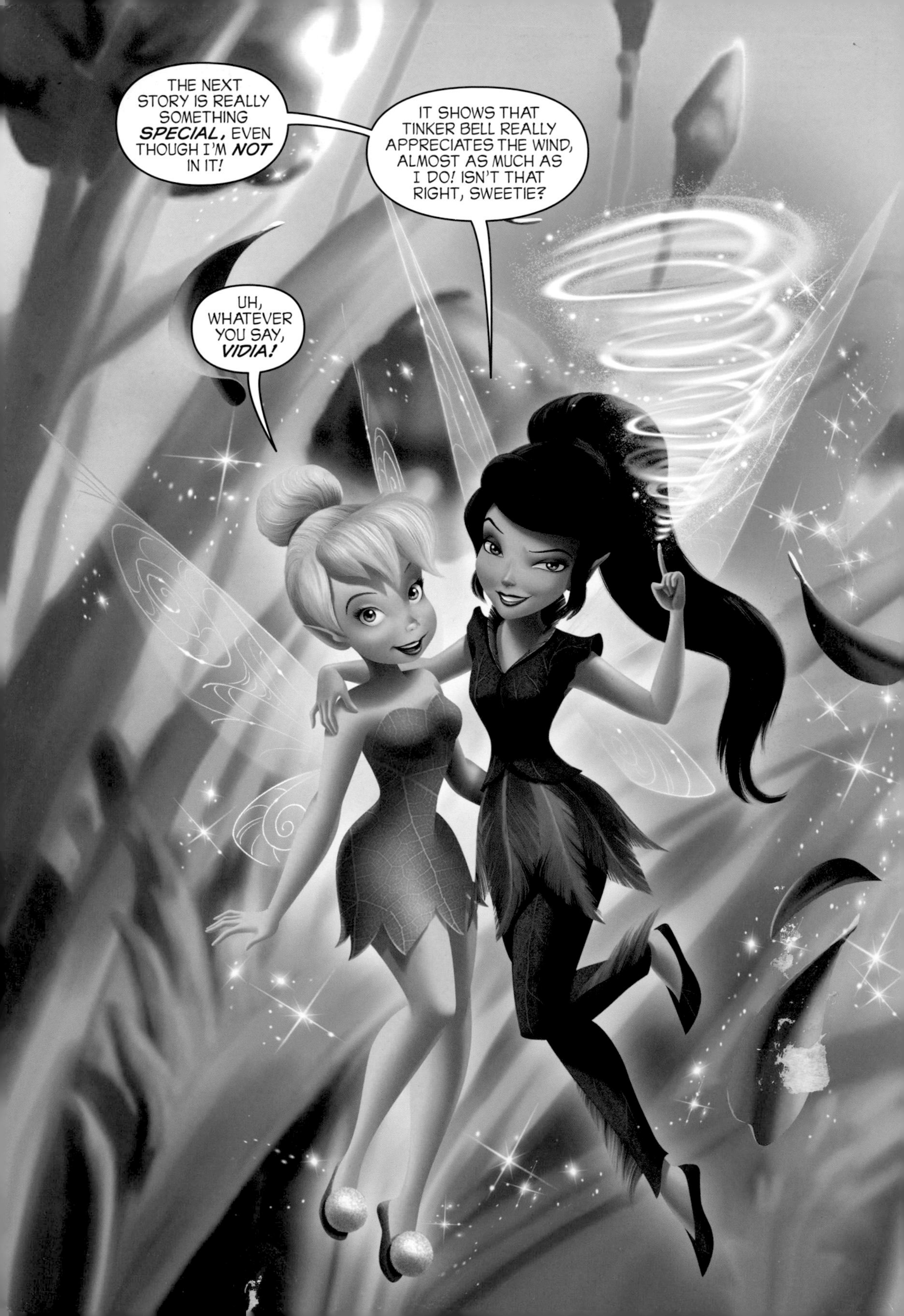
THE NEXT STORY IS REALLY SOMETHING **SPECIAL,** EVEN THOUGH I'M **NOT** IN IT!
IT SHOWS THAT TINKER BELL REALLY APPRECIATES THE WIND, ALMOST AS MUCH AS I DO! ISN'T THAT RIGHT, SWEETIE?
UH, WHATEVER YOU SAY, **VIDIA!**

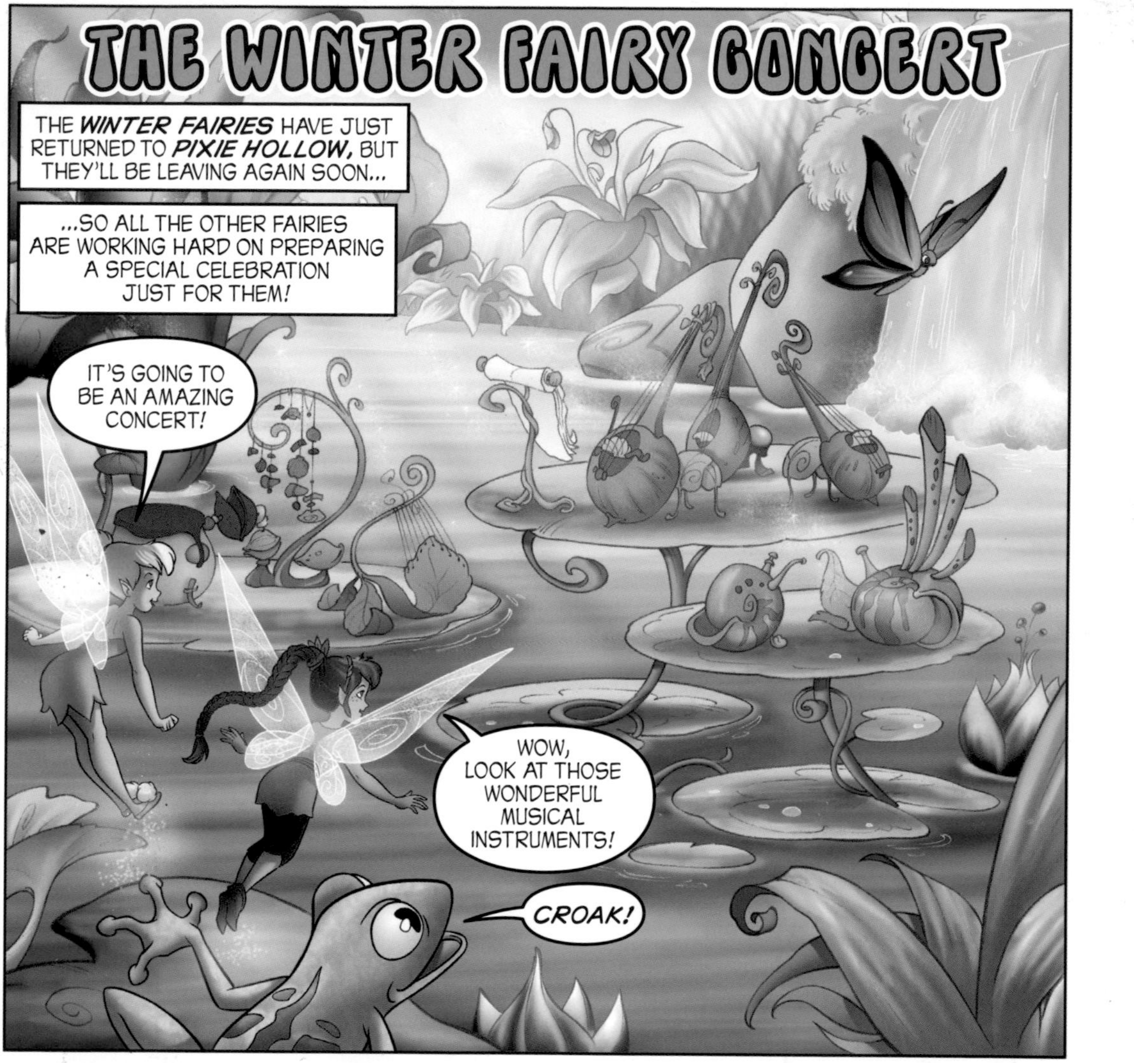
THE WINTER FAIRY CONCERT
THE WINTER FAIRIES HAVE JUST RETURNED TO PIXIE HOLLOW, BUT THEY'LL BE LEAVING AGAIN SOON...
...SO ALL THE OTHER FAIRIES ARE WORKING HARD ON PREPARING A SPECIAL CELEBRATION JUST FOR THEM!
IT'S GOING TO BE AN AMAZING CONCERT!
WOW, LOOK AT THOSE WONDERFUL MUSICAL INSTRUMENTS!
CROAK!

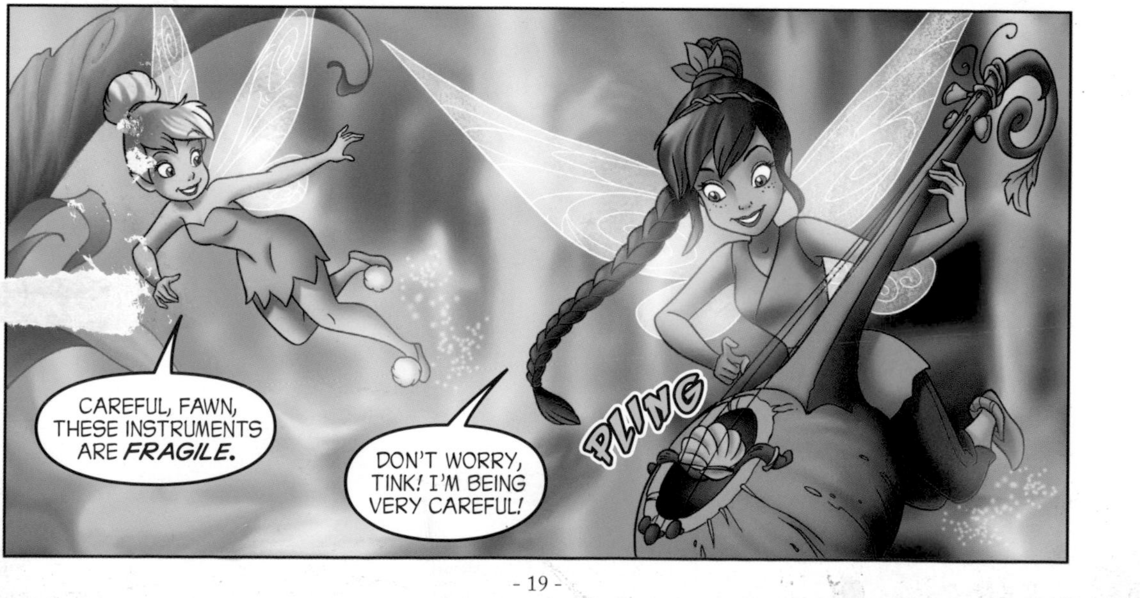
CAREFUL, FAWN, THESE INSTRUMENTS ARE FRAGILE.
DON'T WORRY, TINK! I'M BEING VERY CAREFUL!
PLING

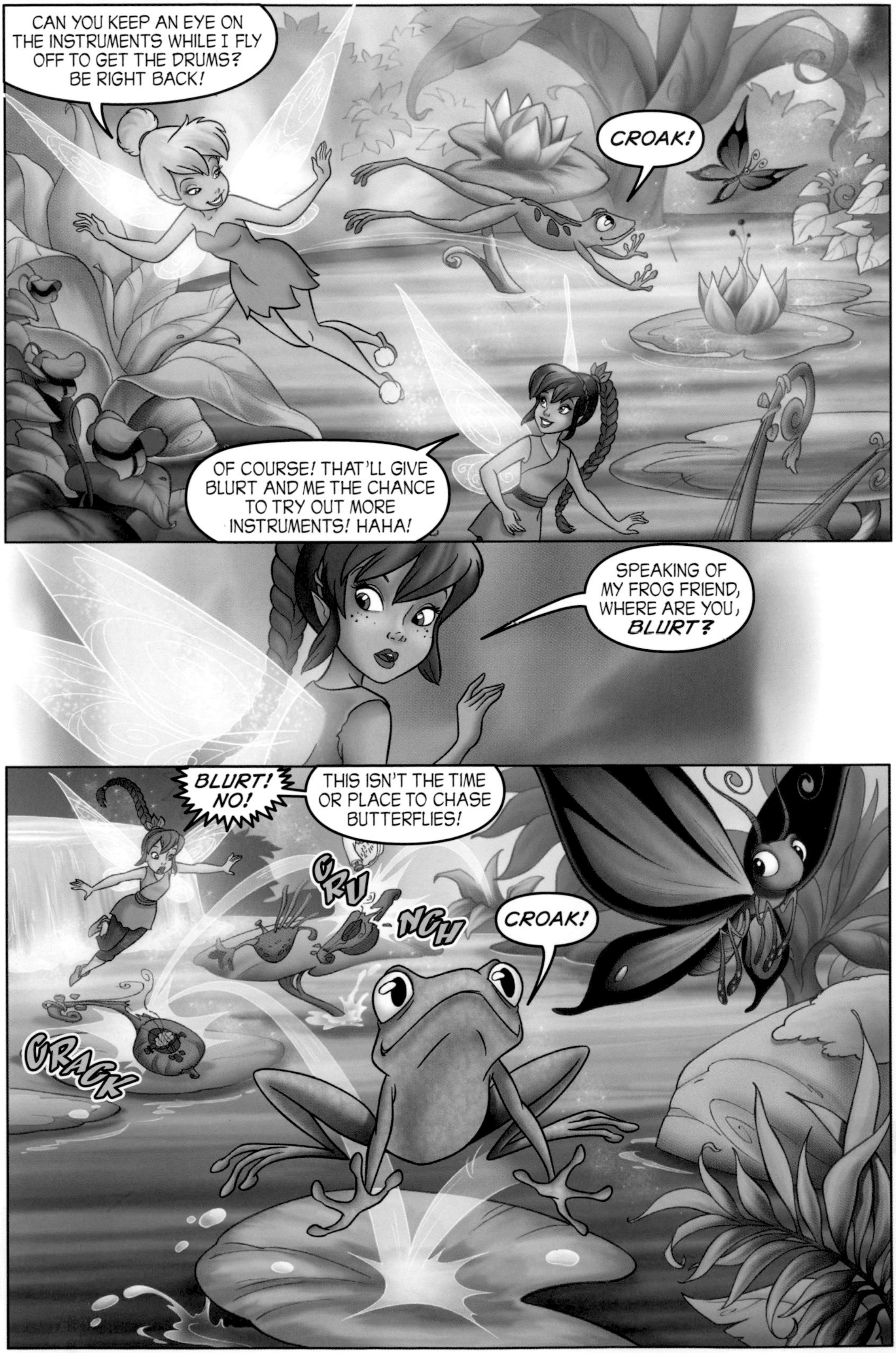
CAN YOU KEEP AN EYE ON THE INSTRUMENTS WHILE I FLY OFF TO GET THE DRUMS? BE RIGHT BACK!
CROAK!
OF COURSE! THAT'LL GIVE BLURT AND ME THE CHANCE TO TRY OUT MORE INSTRUMENTS! HAHA!
SPEAKING OF MY FROG FRIEND, WHERE ARE YOU, BLURT?
BLURT! NO!
THIS ISN'T THE TIME OR PLACE TO CHASE BUTTERFLIES!
CRU-NCH
CROAK!
CRACK

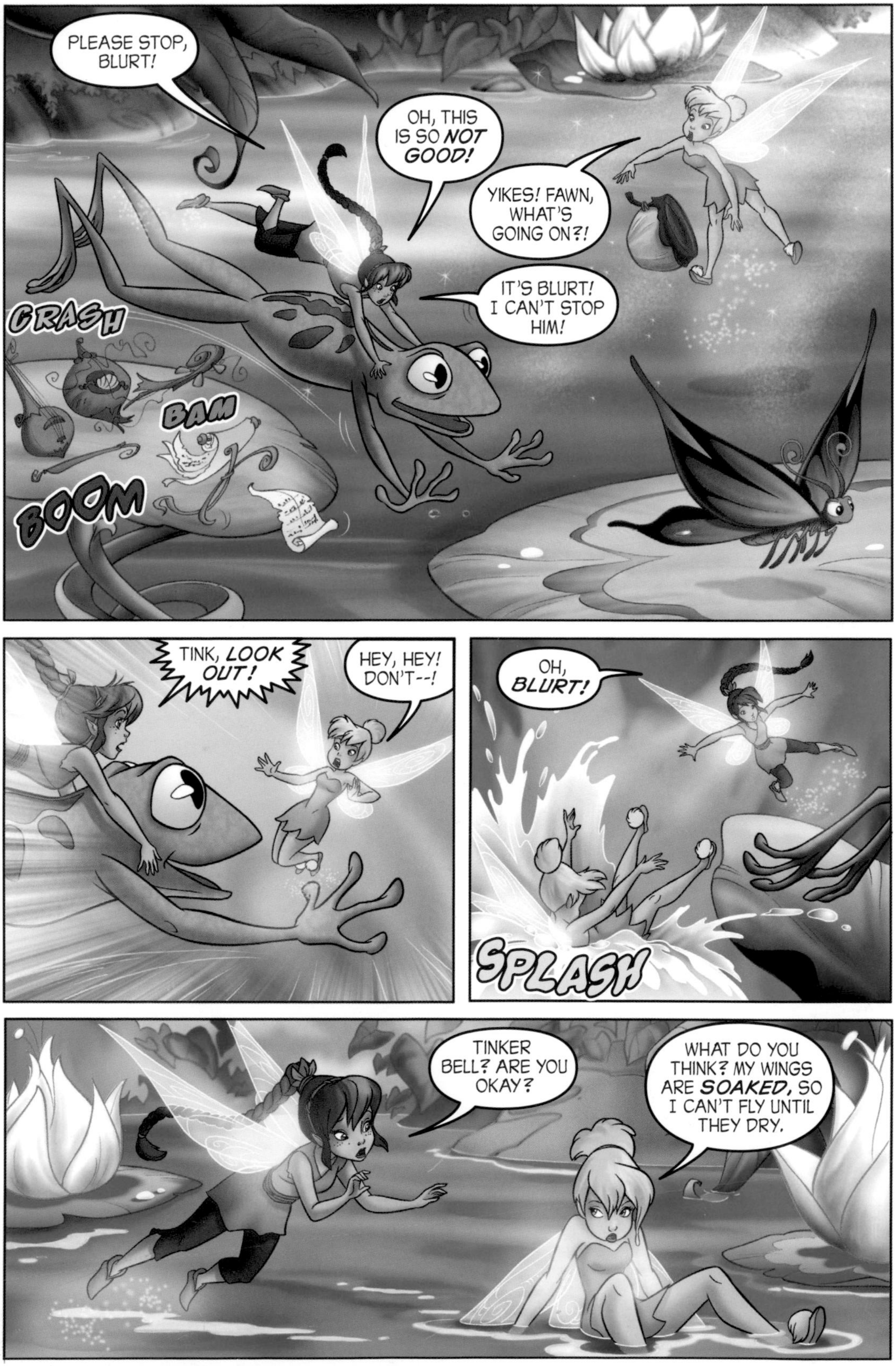
PLEASE STOP, BLURT!
OH, THIS IS SO NOT GOOD!
YIKES! FAWN, WHAT'S GOING ON?!
IT'S BLURT! I CAN'T STOP HIM!
CRASH
BAM
BOOM
TINK, LOOK OUT!
HEY, HEY! DON'T--!
OH, BLURT!
SPLASH
TINKER BELL? ARE YOU OKAY?
WHAT DO YOU THINK? MY WINGS ARE SOAKED, SO I CAN'T FLY UNTIL THEY DRY.

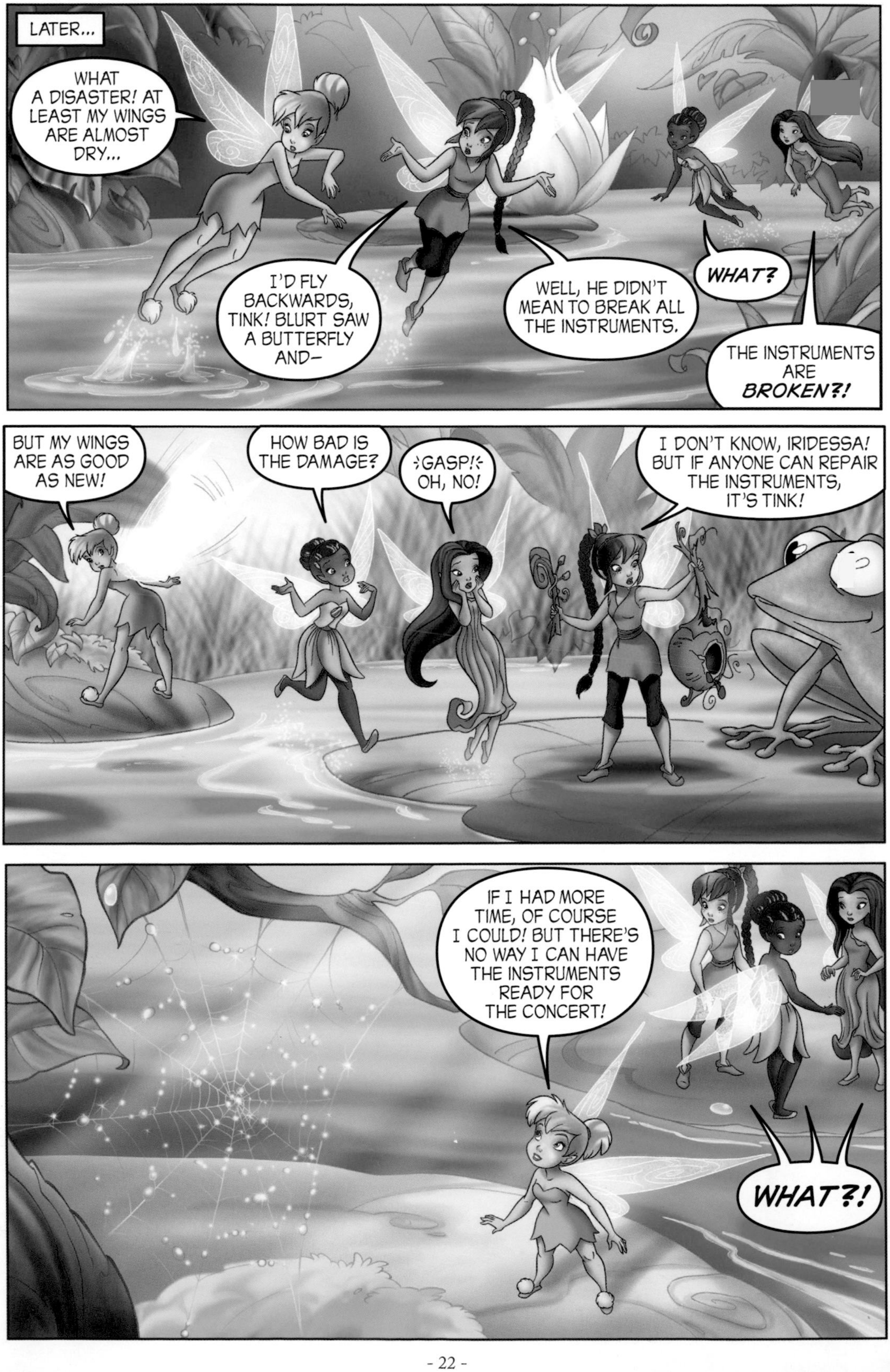
LATER...
WHAT A DISASTER! AT LEAST MY WINGS ARE ALMOST DRY...
I'D FLY BACKWARDS, TINK! BLURT SAW A BUTTERFLY AND–
WELL, HE DIDN'T MEAN TO BREAK ALL THE INSTRUMENTS.
WHAT?
THE INSTRUMENTS ARE BROKEN?!
BUT MY WINGS ARE AS GOOD AS NEW!
HOW BAD IS THE DAMAGE?
GASP! OH, NO!
I DON'T KNOW, IRIDESSA! BUT IF ANYONE CAN REPAIR THE INSTRUMENTS, IT'S TINK!
IF I HAD MORE TIME, OF COURSE I COULD! BUT THERE'S NO WAY I CAN HAVE THE INSTRUMENTS READY FOR THE CONCERT!
WHAT?!

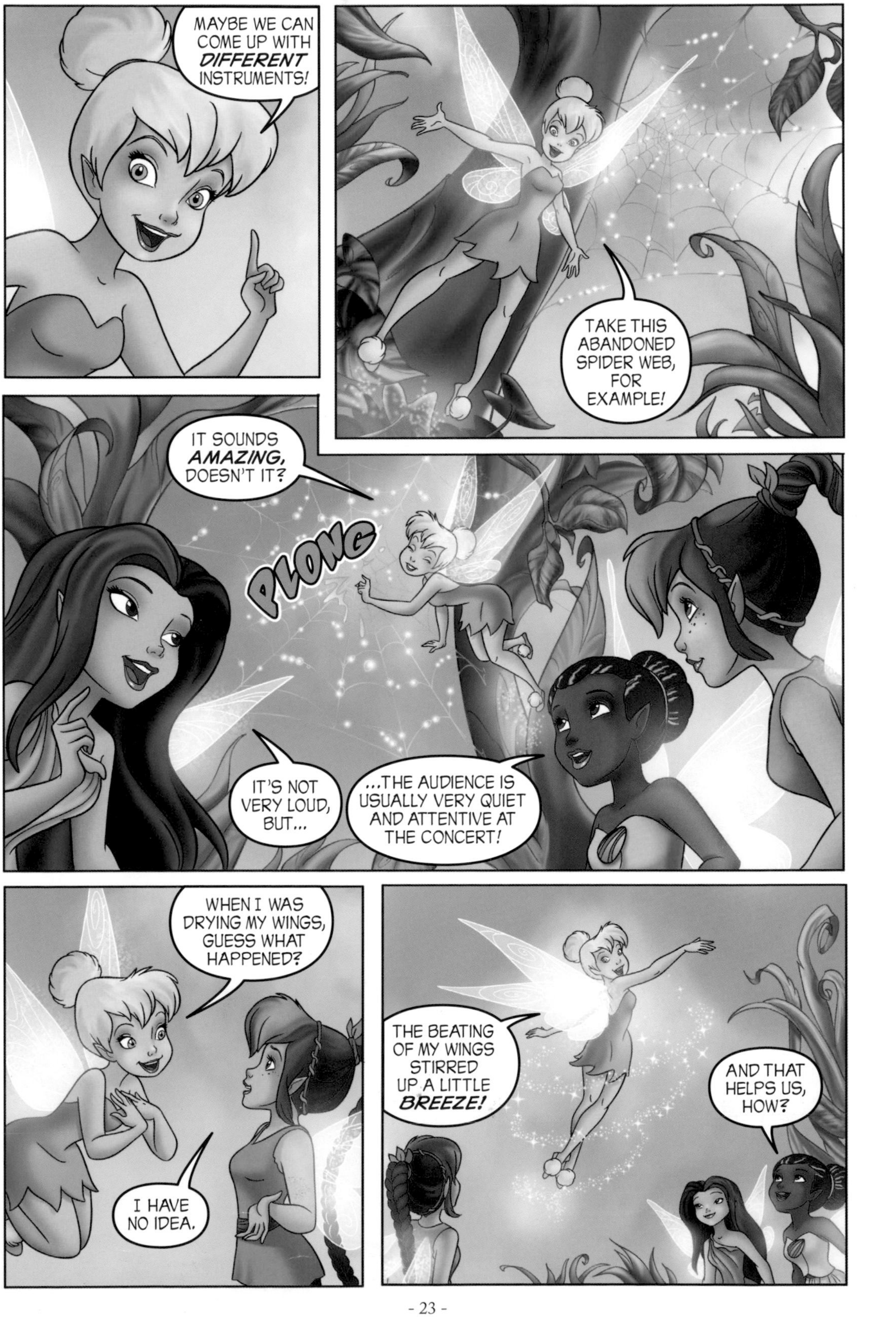
MAYBE WE CAN COME UP WITH *DIFFERENT* INSTRUMENTS!
TAKE THIS ABANDONED SPIDER WEB, FOR EXAMPLE!
IT SOUNDS **AMAZING,** DOESN'T IT?
PLONG
IT'S NOT VERY LOUD, BUT...
...THE AUDIENCE IS USUALLY VERY QUIET AND ATTENTIVE AT THE CONCERT!
WHEN I WAS DRYING MY WINGS, GUESS WHAT HAPPENED?
I HAVE NO IDEA.
THE BEATING OF MY WINGS STIRRED UP A LITTLE *BREEZE!*
AND THAT HELPS US, HOW?

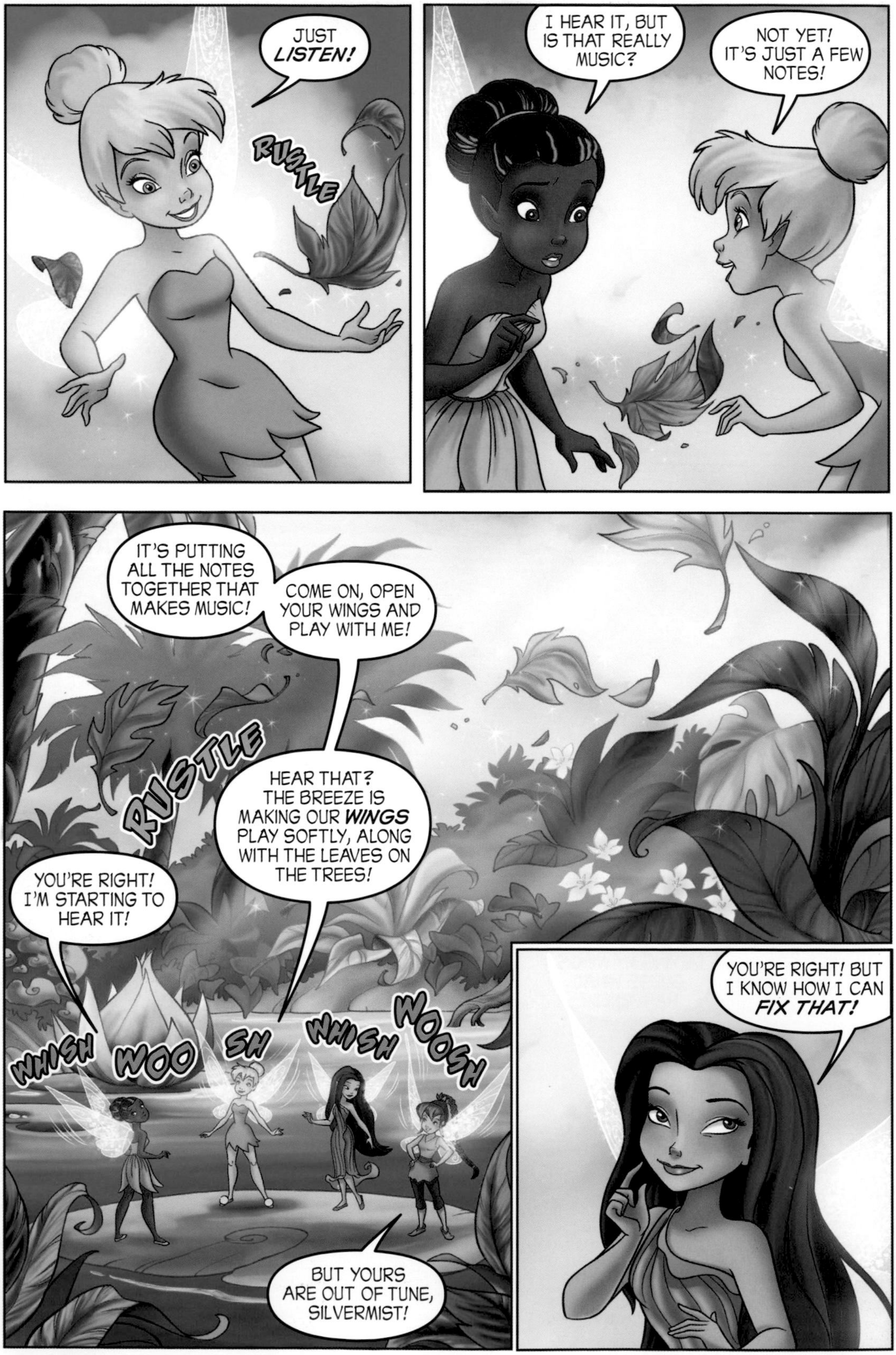
JUST *LISTEN!*
RUSTLE
I HEAR IT, BUT IS THAT REALLY MUSIC?
NOT YET! IT'S JUST A FEW NOTES!
IT'S PUTTING ALL THE NOTES TOGETHER THAT MAKES MUSIC!
COME ON, OPEN YOUR WINGS AND PLAY WITH ME!
RUSTLE
HEAR THAT? THE BREEZE IS MAKING OUR ***WINGS*** PLAY SOFTLY, ALONG WITH THE LEAVES ON THE TREES!
YOU'RE RIGHT! I'M STARTING TO HEAR IT!
WHISH WOO SH WHISH WOOSH
BUT YOURS ARE OUT OF TUNE, SILVERMIST!
YOU'RE RIGHT! BUT I KNOW HOW I CAN ***FIX THAT!***

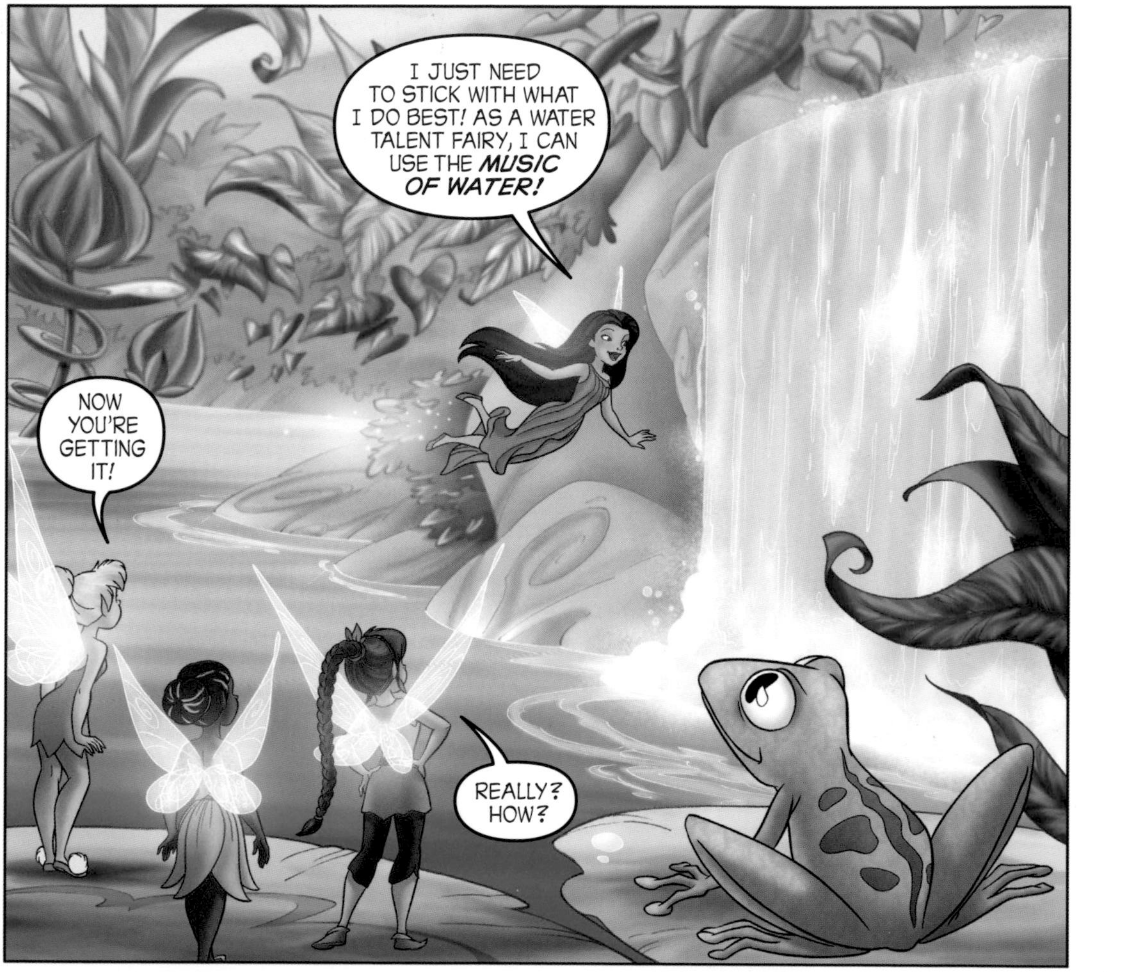
I JUST NEED TO STICK WITH WHAT I DO BEST! AS A WATER TALENT FAIRY, I CAN USE THE *MUSIC OF WATER!*
NOW YOU'RE GETTING IT!
REALLY? HOW?

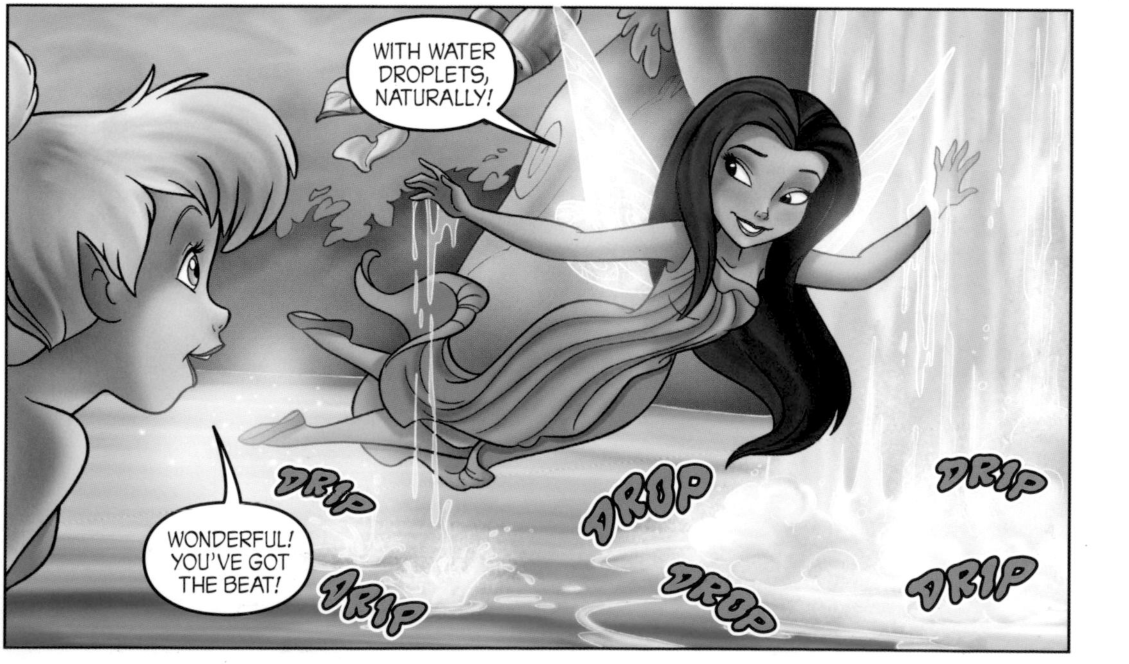
WITH WATER DROPLETS, NATURALLY!
WONDERFUL! YOU'VE GOT THE BEAT!
DRIP
DRIP
DROP
DROP
DRIP
DRIP

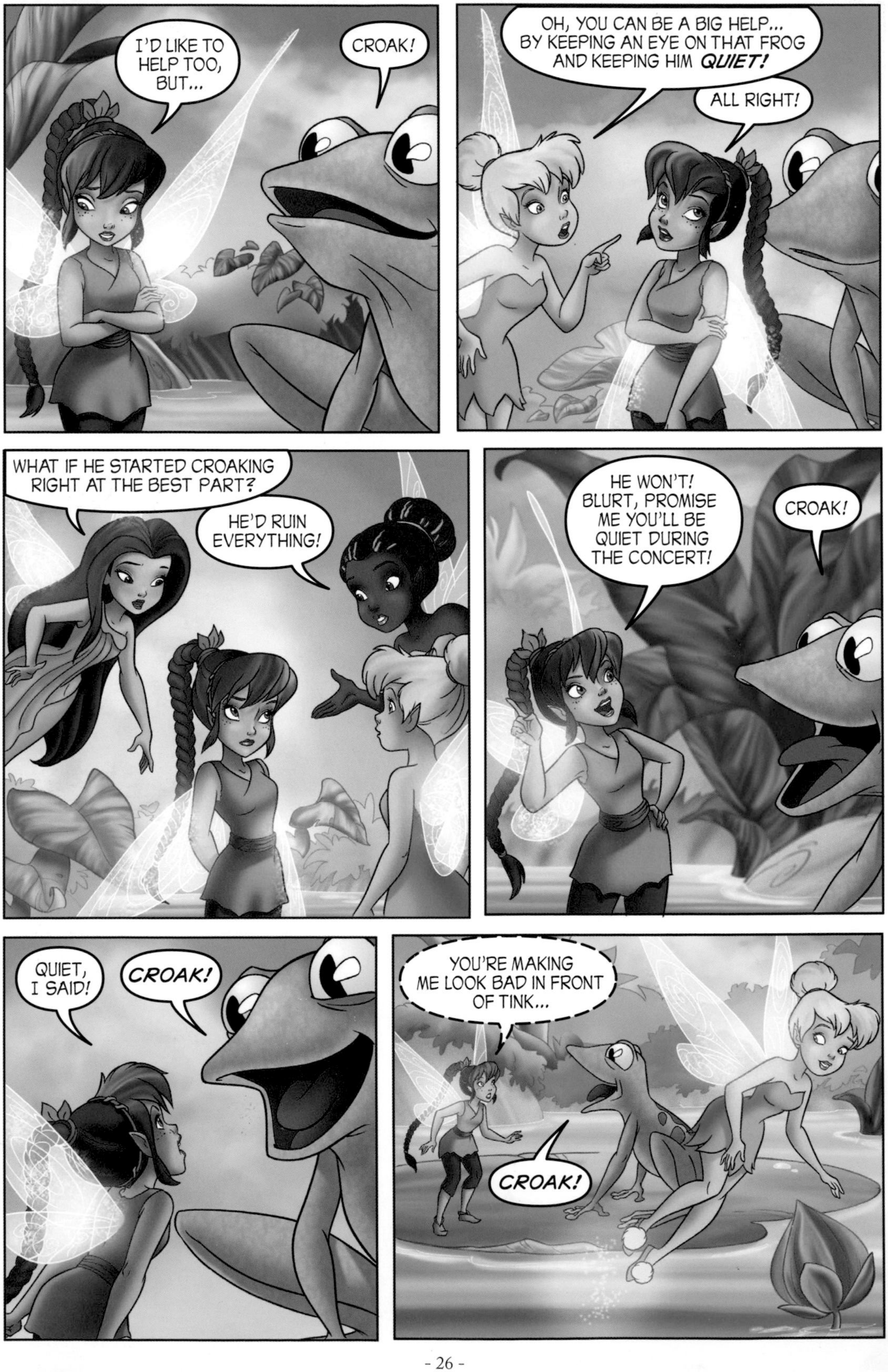
I'D LIKE TO HELP TOO, BUT...
CROAK!
OH, YOU CAN BE A BIG HELP... BY KEEPING AN EYE ON THAT FROG AND KEEPING HIM *QUIET!*
ALL RIGHT!
WHAT IF HE STARTED CROAKING RIGHT AT THE BEST PART?
HE'D RUIN EVERYTHING!
HE WON'T! BLURT, PROMISE ME YOU'LL BE QUIET DURING THE CONCERT!
CROAK!
QUIET, I SAID!
CROAK!
YOU'RE MAKING ME LOOK BAD IN FRONT OF TINK...
CROAK!

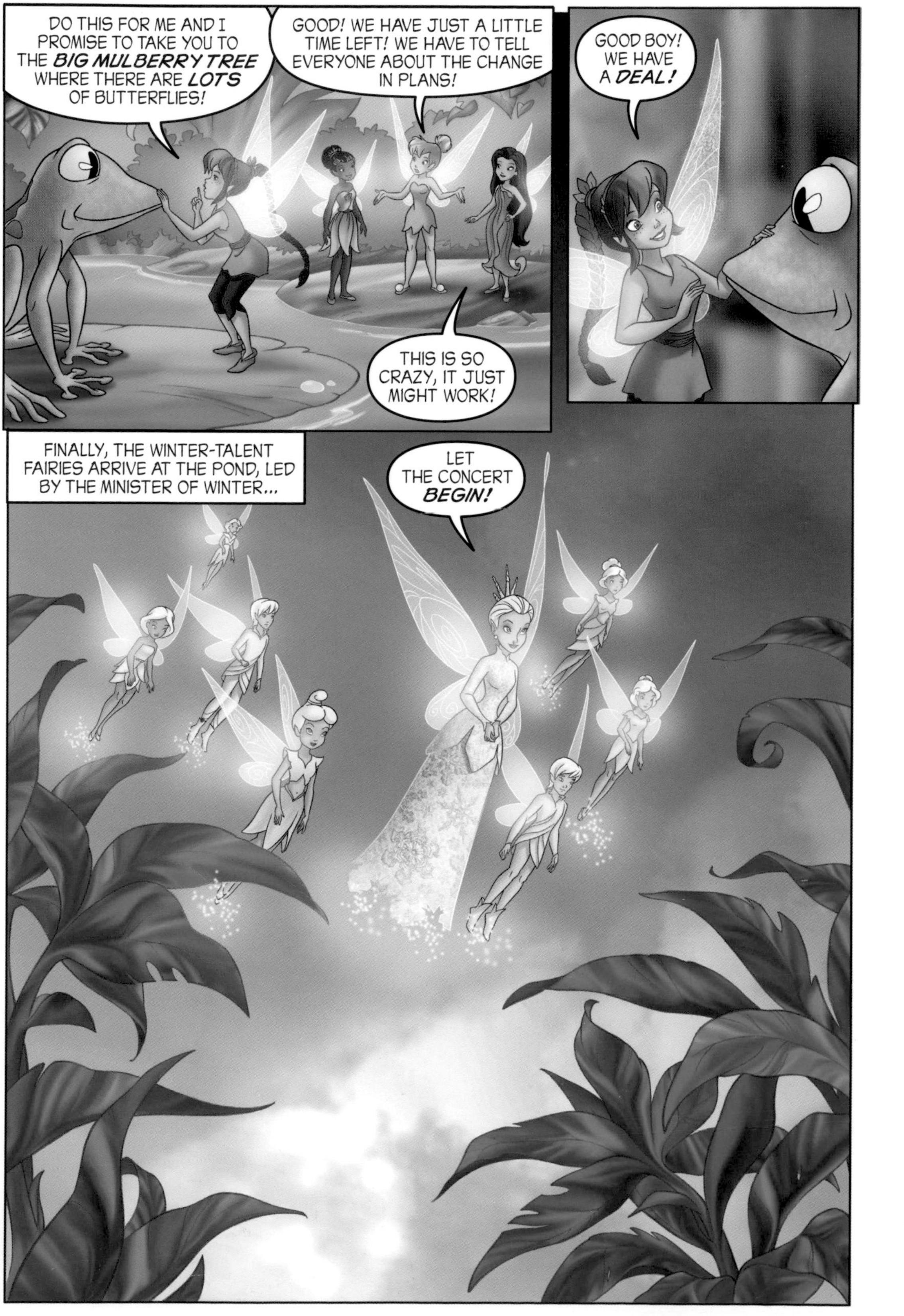
DO THIS FOR ME AND I PROMISE TO TAKE YOU TO THE BIG MULBERRY TREE WHERE THERE ARE LOTS OF BUTTERFLIES!
GOOD! WE HAVE JUST A LITTLE TIME LEFT! WE HAVE TO TELL EVERYONE ABOUT THE CHANGE IN PLANS!
THIS IS SO CRAZY, IT JUST MIGHT WORK!
GOOD BOY! WE HAVE A DEAL!
FINALLY, THE WINTER-TALENT FAIRIES ARRIVE AT THE POND, LED BY THE MINISTER OF WINTER...
LET THE CONCERT BEGIN!

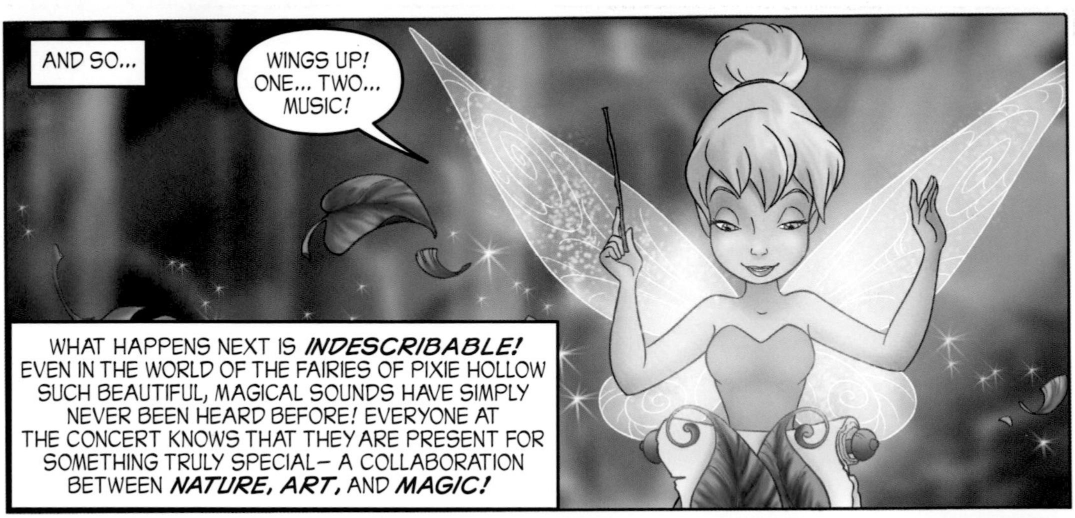
AND SO...
WINGS UP! ONE... TWO... MUSIC!
WHAT HAPPENS NEXT IS *INDESCRIBABLE!* EVEN IN THE WORLD OF THE FAIRIES OF PIXIE HOLLOW SUCH BEAUTIFUL, MAGICAL SOUNDS HAVE SIMPLY NEVER BEEN HEARD BEFORE! EVERYONE AT THE CONCERT KNOWS THAT THEY ARE PRESENT FOR SOMETHING TRULY SPECIAL– A COLLABORATION BETWEEN *NATURE, ART,* AND *MAGIC!*

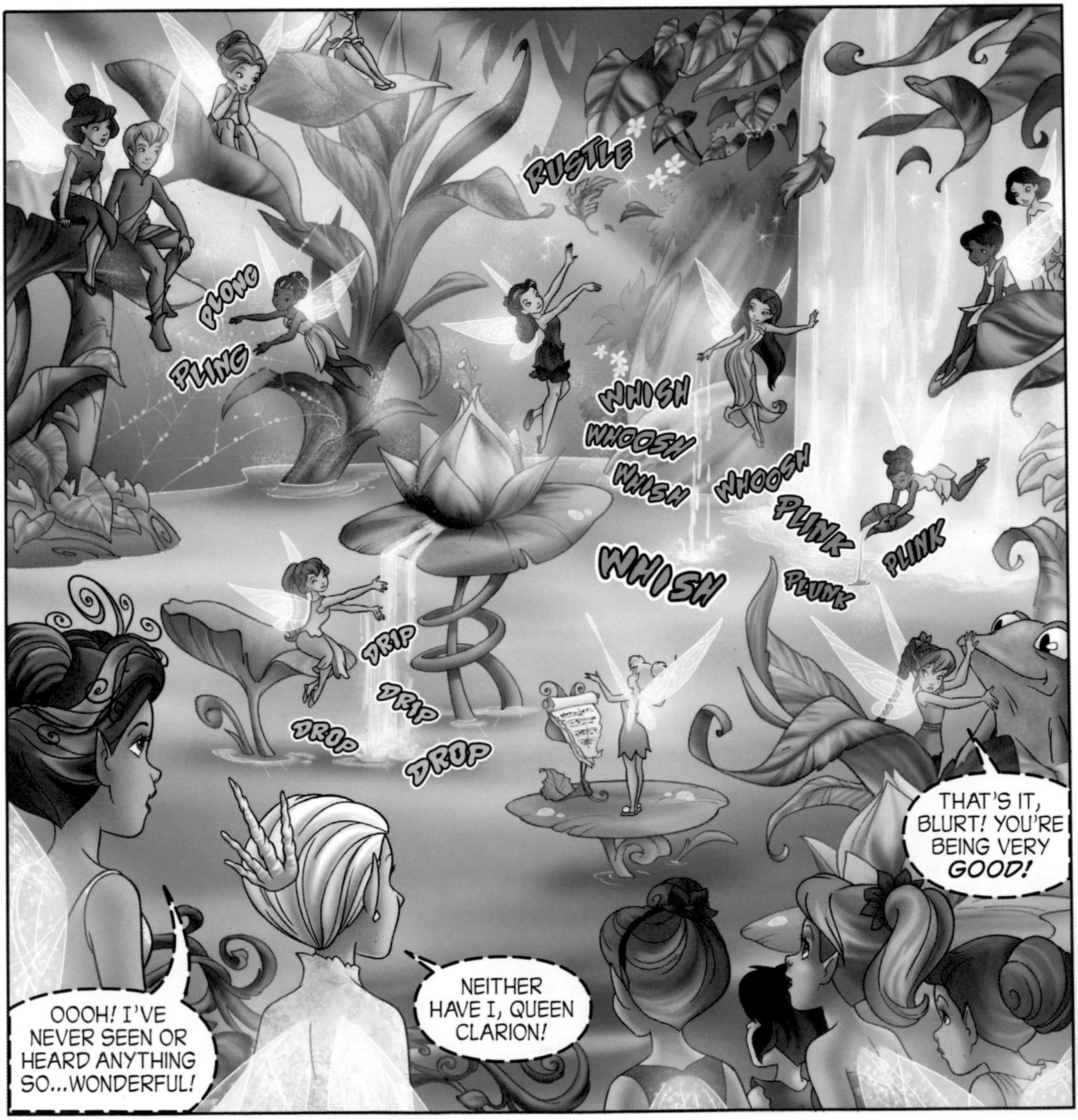
RUSTLE
PLONG
PLING
WHISH
WHOOSH
WHISH
WHOOSH
PLINK
PLINK
WHISH
PLUNK
DRIP
DRIP
DROP
DROP
THAT'S IT, BLURT! YOU'RE BEING VERY *GOOD!*
OOOH! I'VE NEVER SEEN OR HEARD ANYTHING SO...WONDERFUL!
NEITHER HAVE I, QUEEN CLARION!

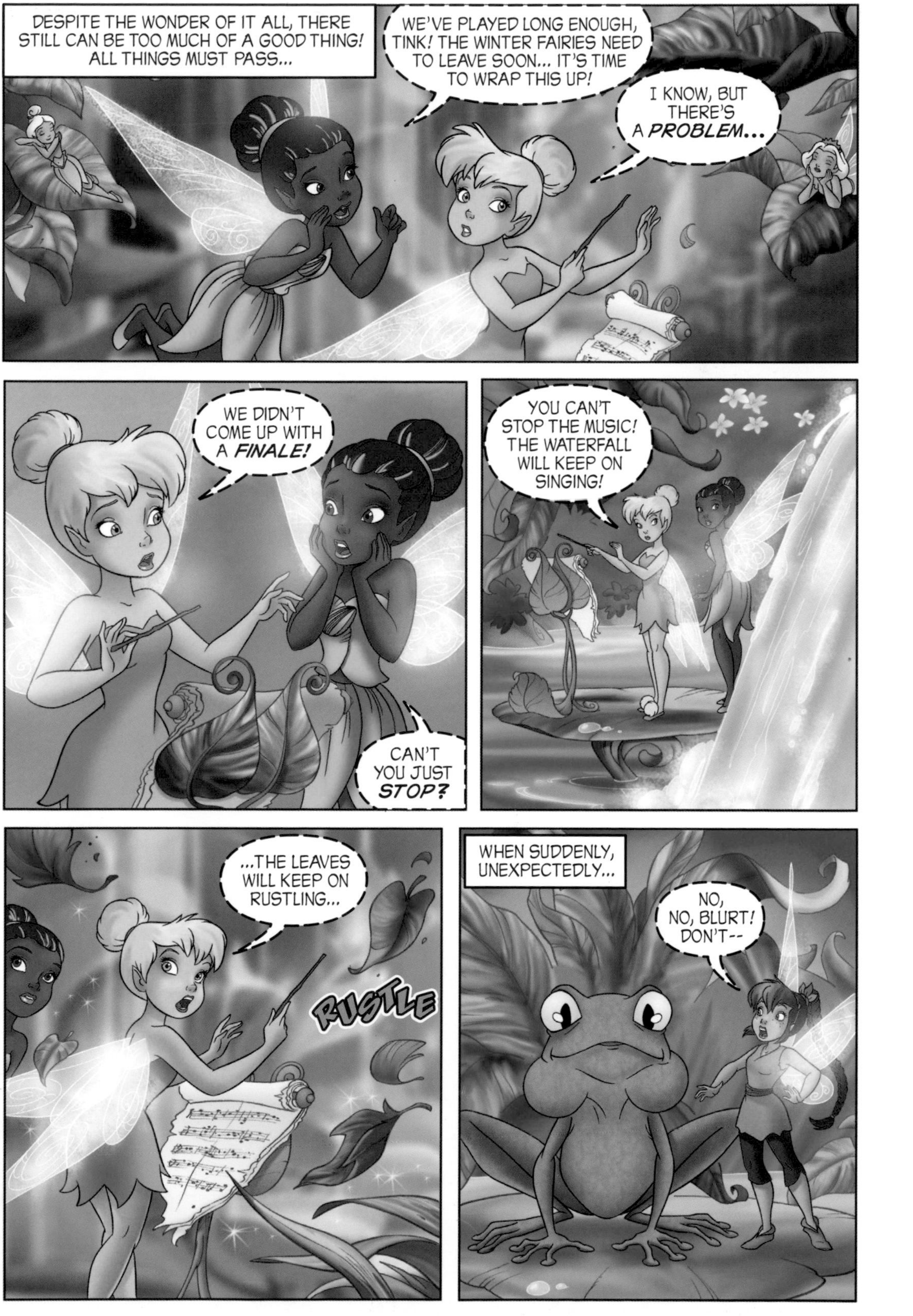

DESPITE THE WONDER OF IT ALL, THERE STILL CAN BE TOO MUCH OF A GOOD THING! ALL THINGS MUST PASS...
WE'VE PLAYED LONG ENOUGH, TINK! THE WINTER FAIRIES NEED TO LEAVE SOON... IT'S TIME TO WRAP THIS UP!
I KNOW, BUT THERE'S A PROBLEM...
WE DIDN'T COME UP WITH A FINALE!
CAN'T YOU JUST STOP?
YOU CAN'T STOP THE MUSIC! THE WATERFALL WILL KEEP ON SINGING!
...THE LEAVES WILL KEEP ON RUSTLING...
RUSTLE
WHEN SUDDENLY, UNEXPECTEDLY...
NO, NO, BLURT! DON'T--

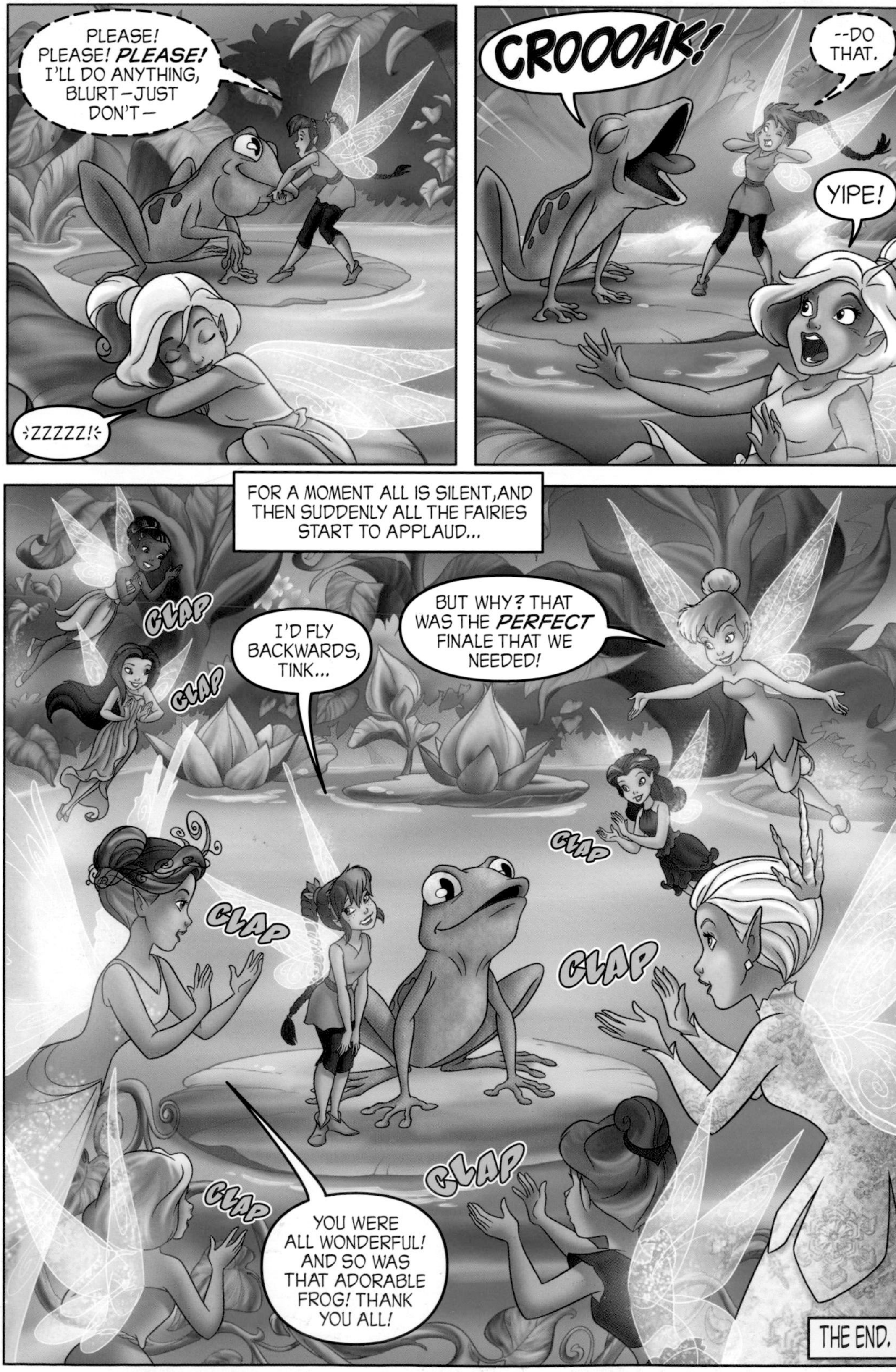
PLEASE! PLEASE! ***PLEASE!*** I'LL DO ANYTHING, BLURT—JUST DON'T—
ZZZZZ!
CROOOAK!
--DO THAT.
YIPE!
FOR A MOMENT ALL IS SILENT, AND THEN SUDDENLY ALL THE FAIRIES START TO APPLAUD...
CLAP
CLAP
I'D FLY BACKWARDS, TINK...
BUT WHY? THAT WAS THE ***PERFECT*** FINALE THAT WE NEEDED!
CLAP
CLAP
CLAP
CLAP
CLAP
YOU WERE ALL WONDERFUL! AND SO WAS THAT ADORABLE FROG! THANK YOU ALL!
THE END.

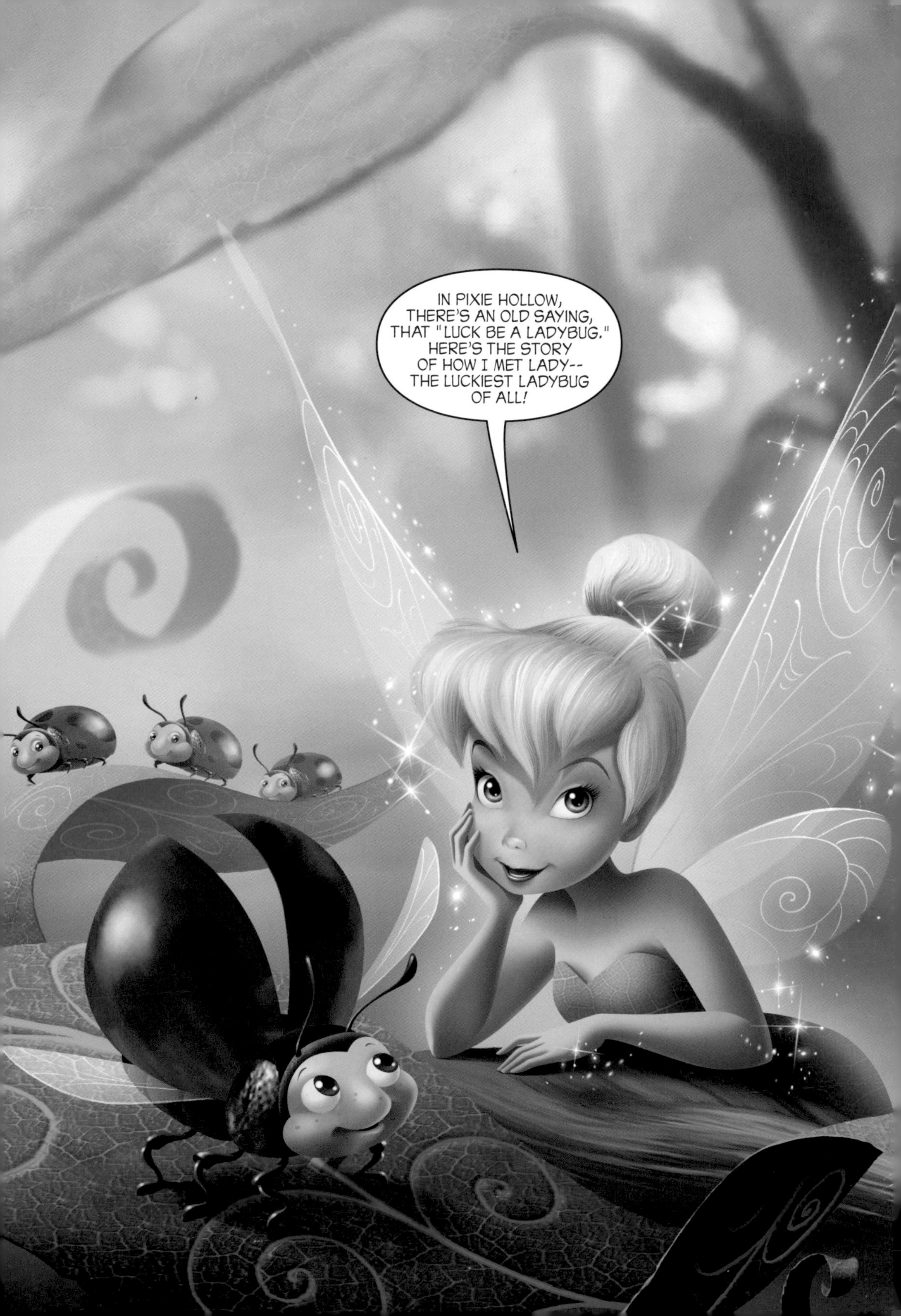
IN PIXIE HOLLOW, THERE'S AN OLD SAYING, THAT "LUCK BE A LADYBUG." HERE'S THE STORY OF HOW I MET LADY-- THE LUCKIEST LADYBUG OF ALL!

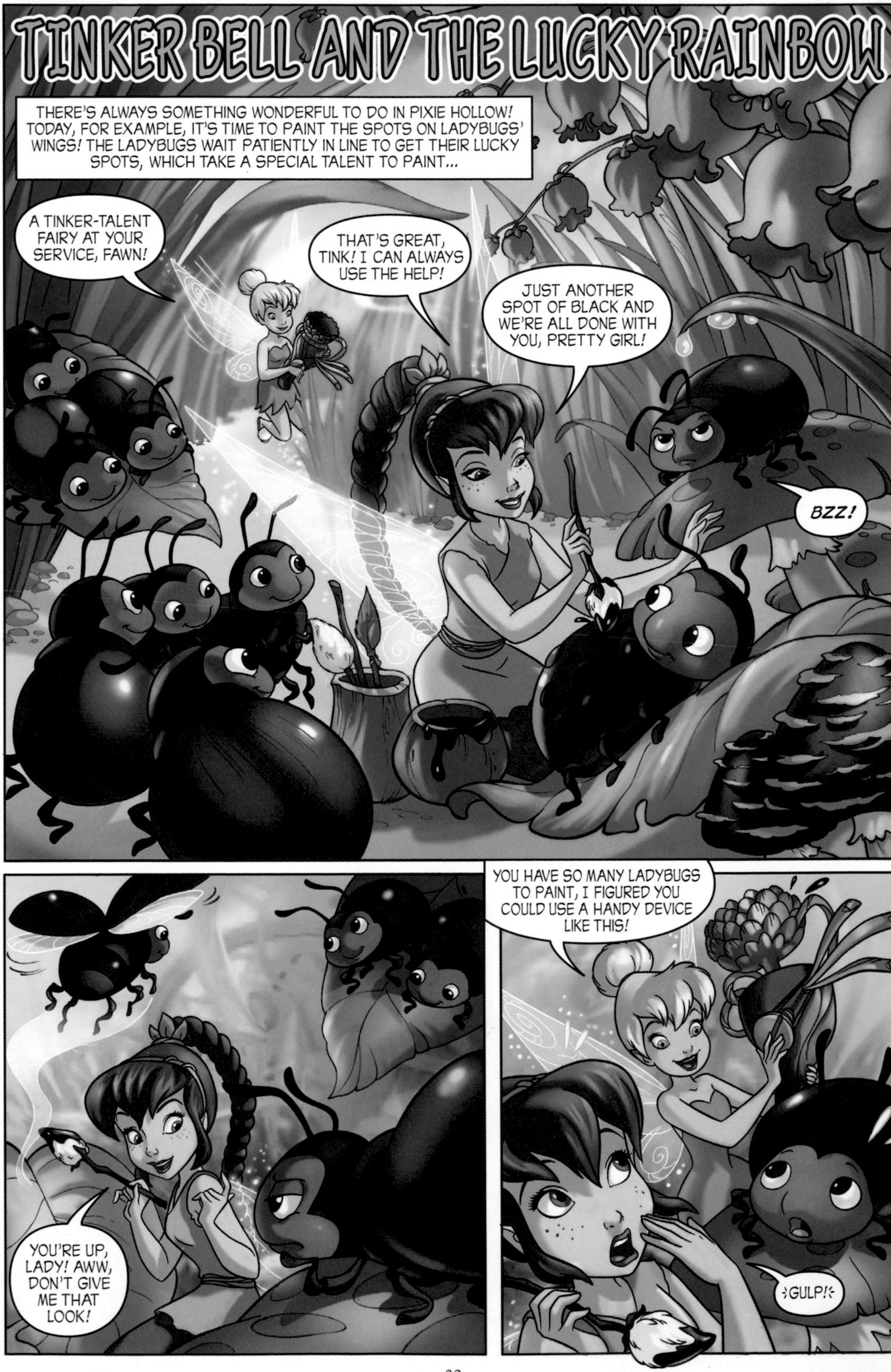
TINKER BELL AND THE LUCKY RAINBOW
THERE'S ALWAYS SOMETHING WONDERFUL TO DO IN PIXIE HOLLOW! TODAY, FOR EXAMPLE, IT'S TIME TO PAINT THE SPOTS ON LADYBUGS' WINGS! THE LADYBUGS WAIT PATIENTLY IN LINE TO GET THEIR LUCKY SPOTS, WHICH TAKE A SPECIAL TALENT TO PAINT...
A TINKER-TALENT FAIRY AT YOUR SERVICE, FAWN!
THAT'S GREAT, TINK! I CAN ALWAYS USE THE HELP!
JUST ANOTHER SPOT OF BLACK AND WE'RE ALL DONE WITH YOU, PRETTY GIRL!
BZZ!
YOU'RE UP, LADY! AWW, DON'T GIVE ME THAT LOOK!
YOU HAVE SO MANY LADYBUGS TO PAINT, I FIGURED YOU COULD USE A HANDY DEVICE LIKE THIS!
GULP!

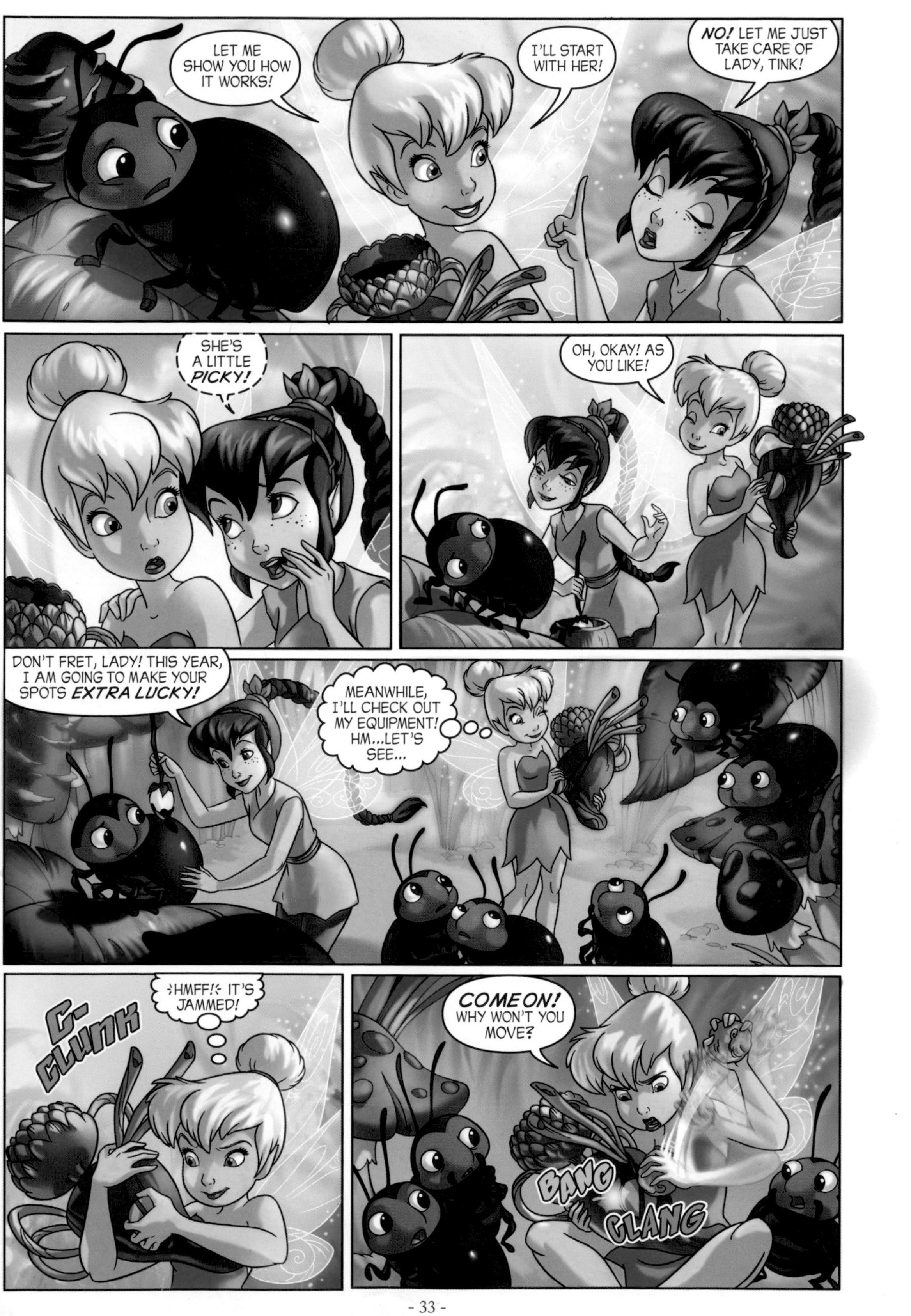
LET ME SHOW YOU HOW IT WORKS!
I'LL START WITH HER!
NO! LET ME JUST TAKE CARE OF LADY, TINK!
SHE'S A LITTLE PICKY!
OH, OKAY! AS YOU LIKE!
DON'T FRET, LADY! THIS YEAR, I AM GOING TO MAKE YOUR SPOTS EXTRA LUCKY!
MEANWHILE, I'LL CHECK OUT MY EQUIPMENT! HM...LET'S SEE...
C-CLUNK
HMFF! IT'S JAMMED!
COME ON! WHY WON'T YOU MOVE?
BANG
CLANG

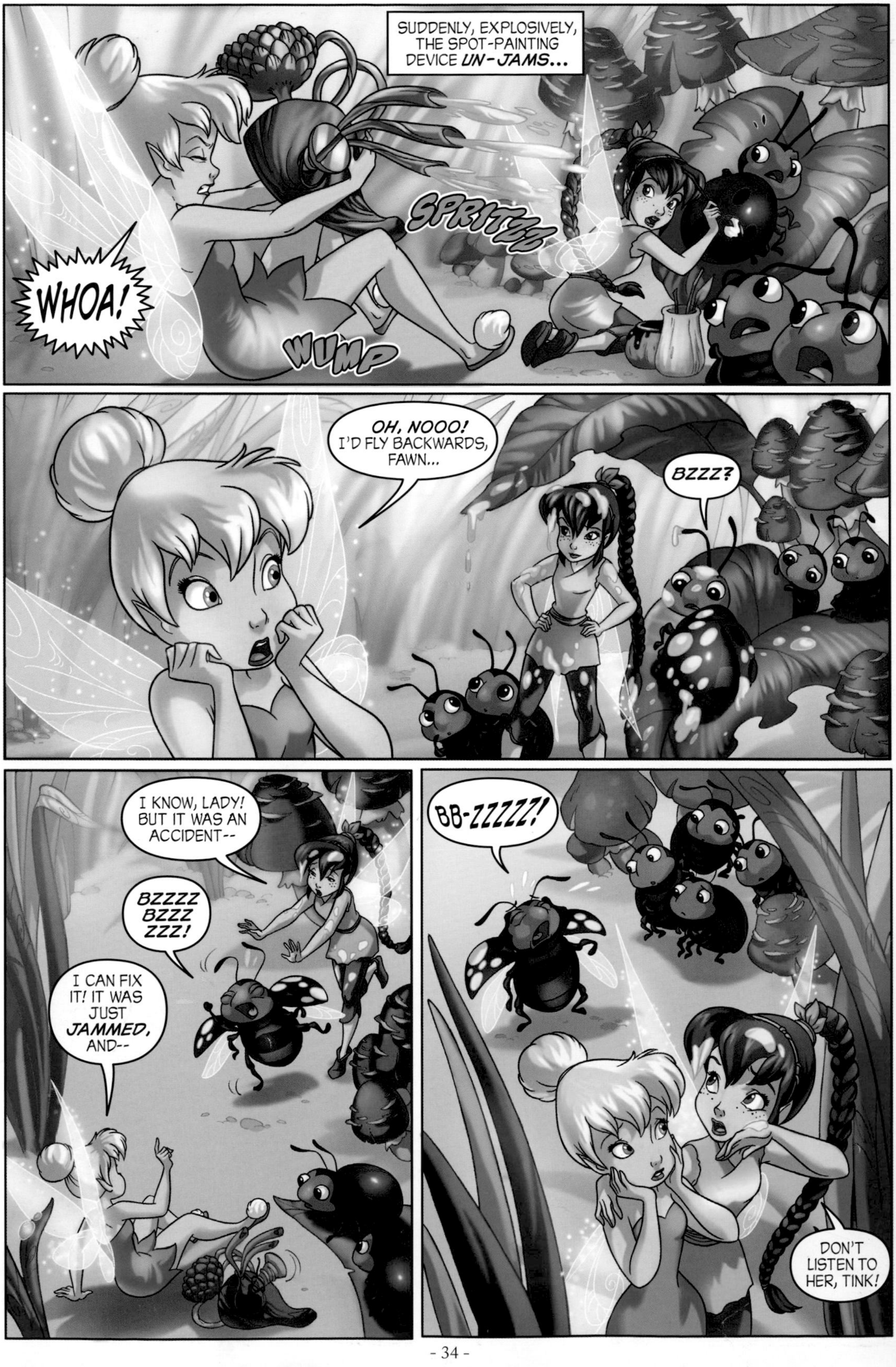

SUDDENLY, EXPLOSIVELY, THE SPOT-PAINTING DEVICE *UN-JAMS...*
SPRITZZZ
WHOA!
WUMP
OH, NOOO! I'D FLY BACKWARDS, FAWN...
BZZZ?
I KNOW, LADY! BUT IT WAS AN ACCIDENT--
BZZZZ BZZZ ZZZ!
I CAN FIX IT! IT WAS JUST ***JAMMED,*** AND--
BB-ZZZZZ!
DON'T LISTEN TO HER, TINK!

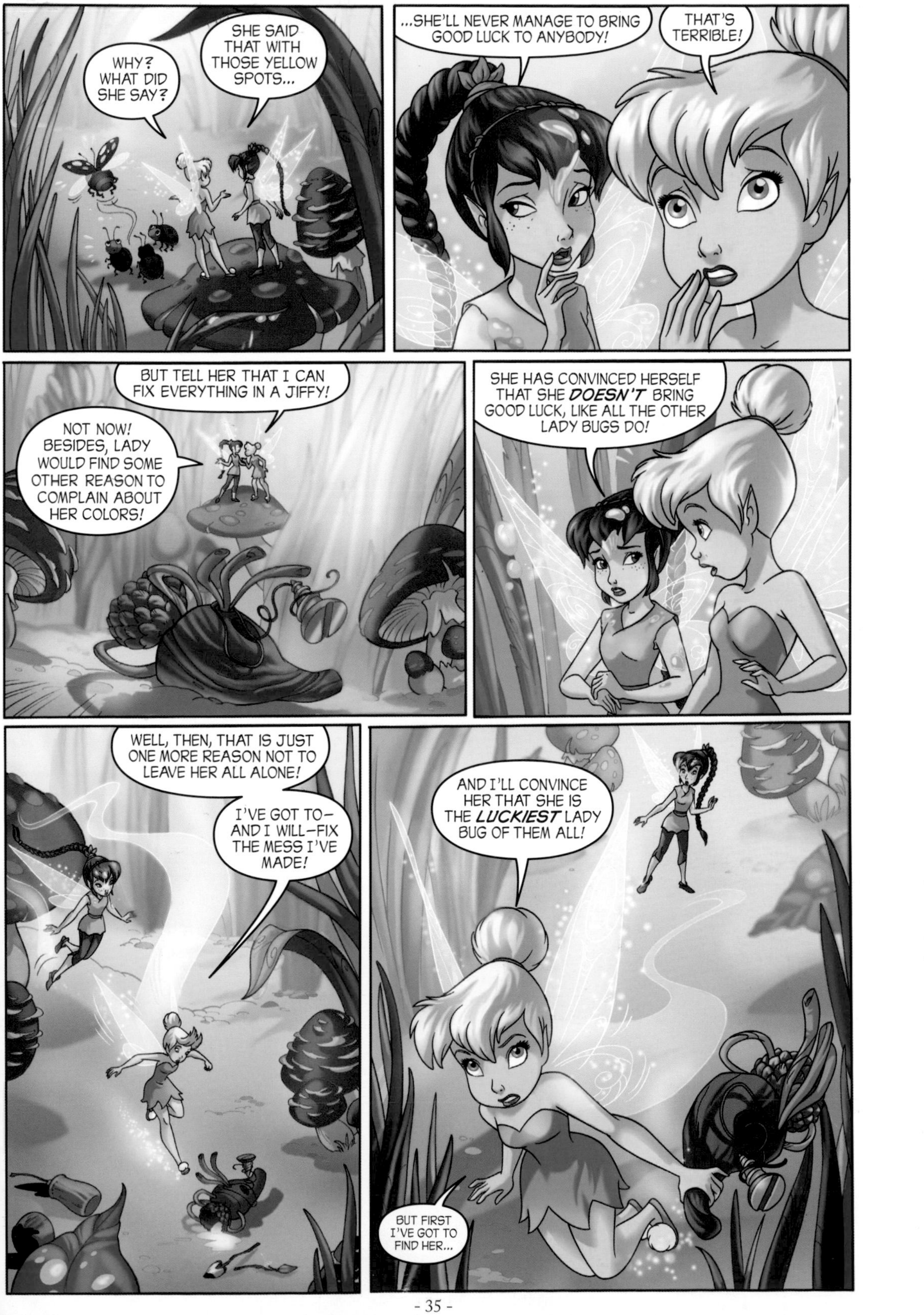
WHY? WHAT DID SHE SAY?
SHE SAID THAT WITH THOSE YELLOW SPOTS...
...SHE'LL NEVER MANAGE TO BRING GOOD LUCK TO ANYBODY!
THAT'S TERRIBLE!
BUT TELL HER THAT I CAN FIX EVERYTHING IN A JIFFY!
NOT NOW! BESIDES, LADY WOULD FIND SOME OTHER REASON TO COMPLAIN ABOUT HER COLORS!
SHE HAS CONVINCED HERSELF THAT SHE DOESN'T BRING GOOD LUCK, LIKE ALL THE OTHER LADY BUGS DO!
WELL, THEN, THAT IS JUST ONE MORE REASON NOT TO LEAVE HER ALL ALONE!
I'VE GOT TO– AND I WILL–FIX THE MESS I'VE MADE!
AND I'LL CONVINCE HER THAT SHE IS THE LUCKIEST LADY BUG OF THEM ALL!
BUT FIRST I'VE GOT TO FIND HER...

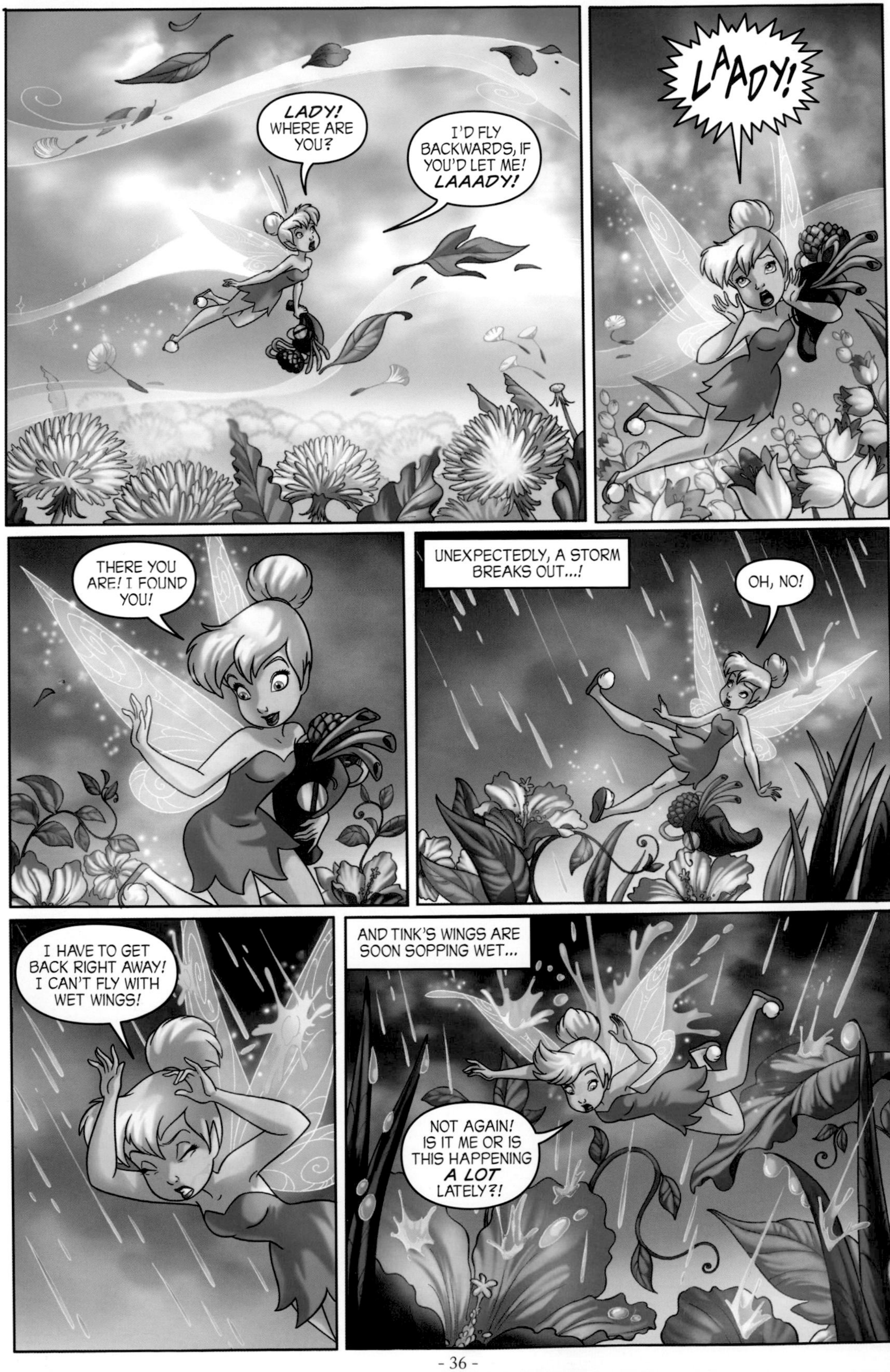
LADY! WHERE ARE YOU?
I'D FLY BACKWARDS, IF YOU'D LET ME! LAAADY!
LAADY!
THERE YOU ARE! I FOUND YOU!
UNEXPECTEDLY, A STORM BREAKS OUT...!
OH, NO!
I HAVE TO GET BACK RIGHT AWAY! I CAN'T FLY WITH WET WINGS!
AND TINK'S WINGS ARE SOON SOPPING WET...
NOT AGAIN! IS IT ME OR IS THIS HAPPENING A LOT LATELY?!

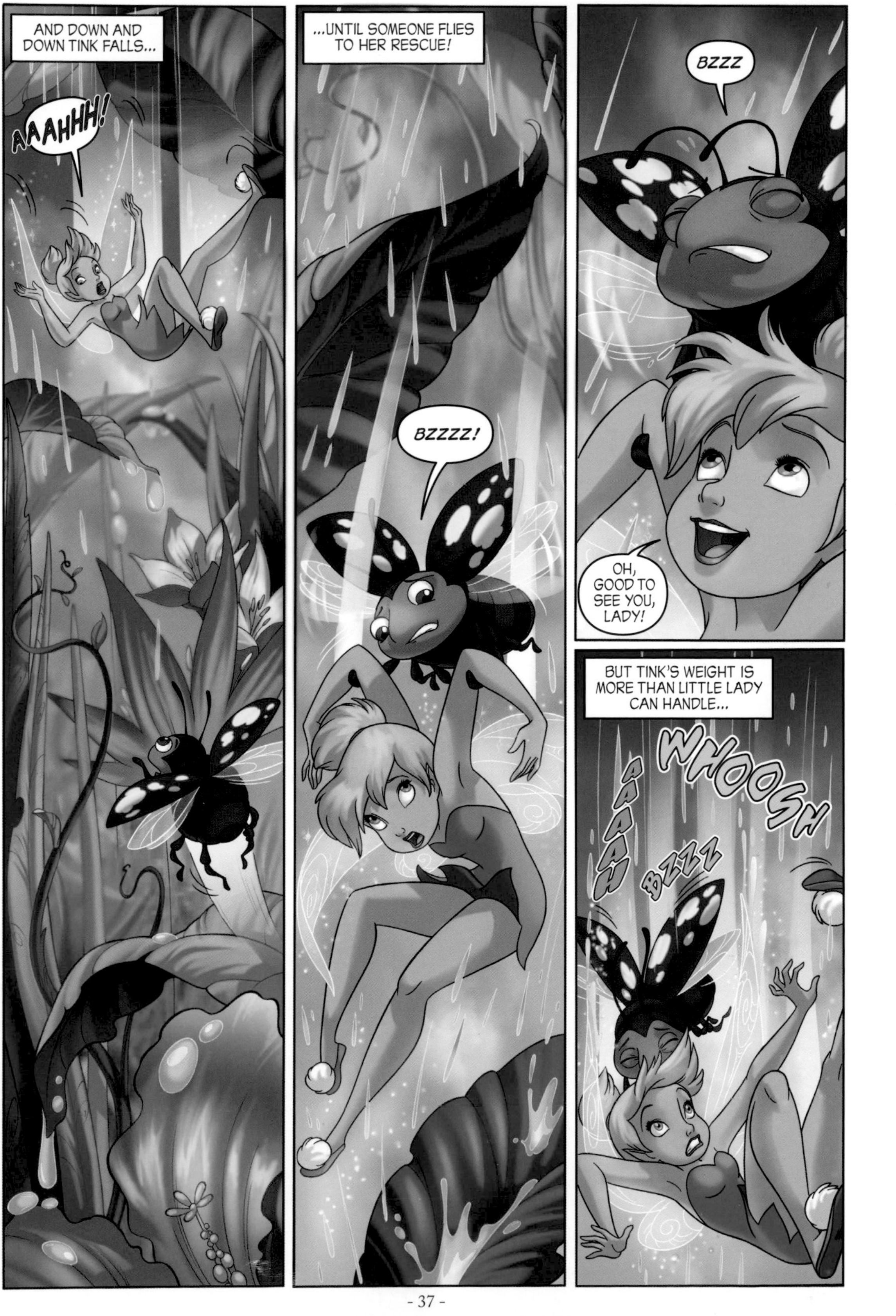

AND DOWN AND DOWN TINK FALLS...
AAAHHH!
...UNTIL SOMEONE FLIES TO HER RESCUE!
BZZZZ!
BZZZ
OH, GOOD TO SEE YOU, LADY!
BUT TINK'S WEIGHT IS MORE THAN LITTLE LADY CAN HANDLE...
WHOOSH
AAAAAH
BZZZ

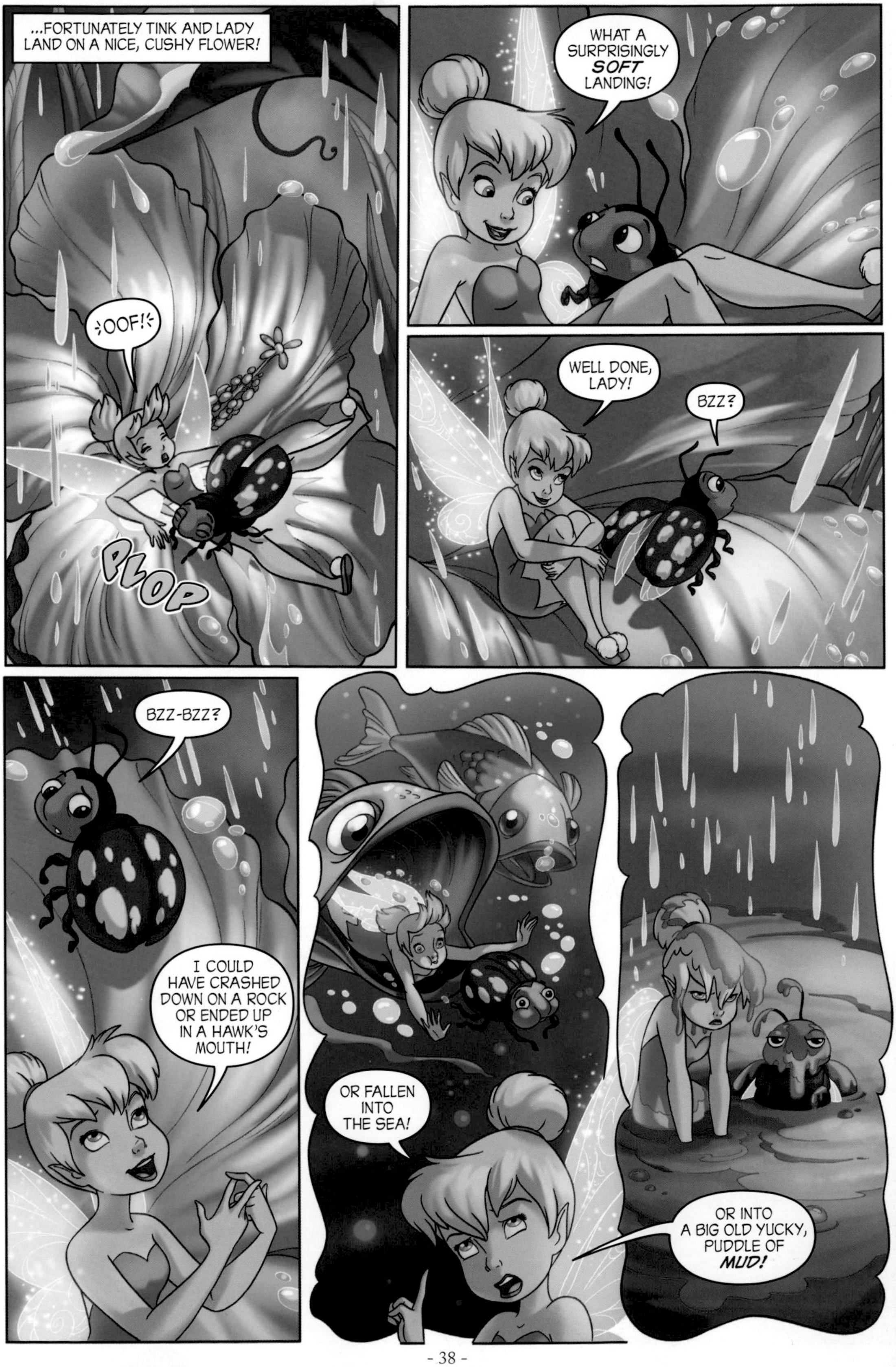
...FORTUNATELY TINK AND LADY LAND ON A NICE, CUSHY FLOWER!
OOF!
PLOP
WHAT A SURPRISINGLY SOFT LANDING!
WELL DONE, LADY!
BZZ?
BZZ-BZZ?
I COULD HAVE CRASHED DOWN ON A ROCK OR ENDED UP IN A HAWK'S MOUTH!
OR FALLEN INTO THE SEA!
OR INTO A BIG OLD YUCKY, PUDDLE OF MUD!

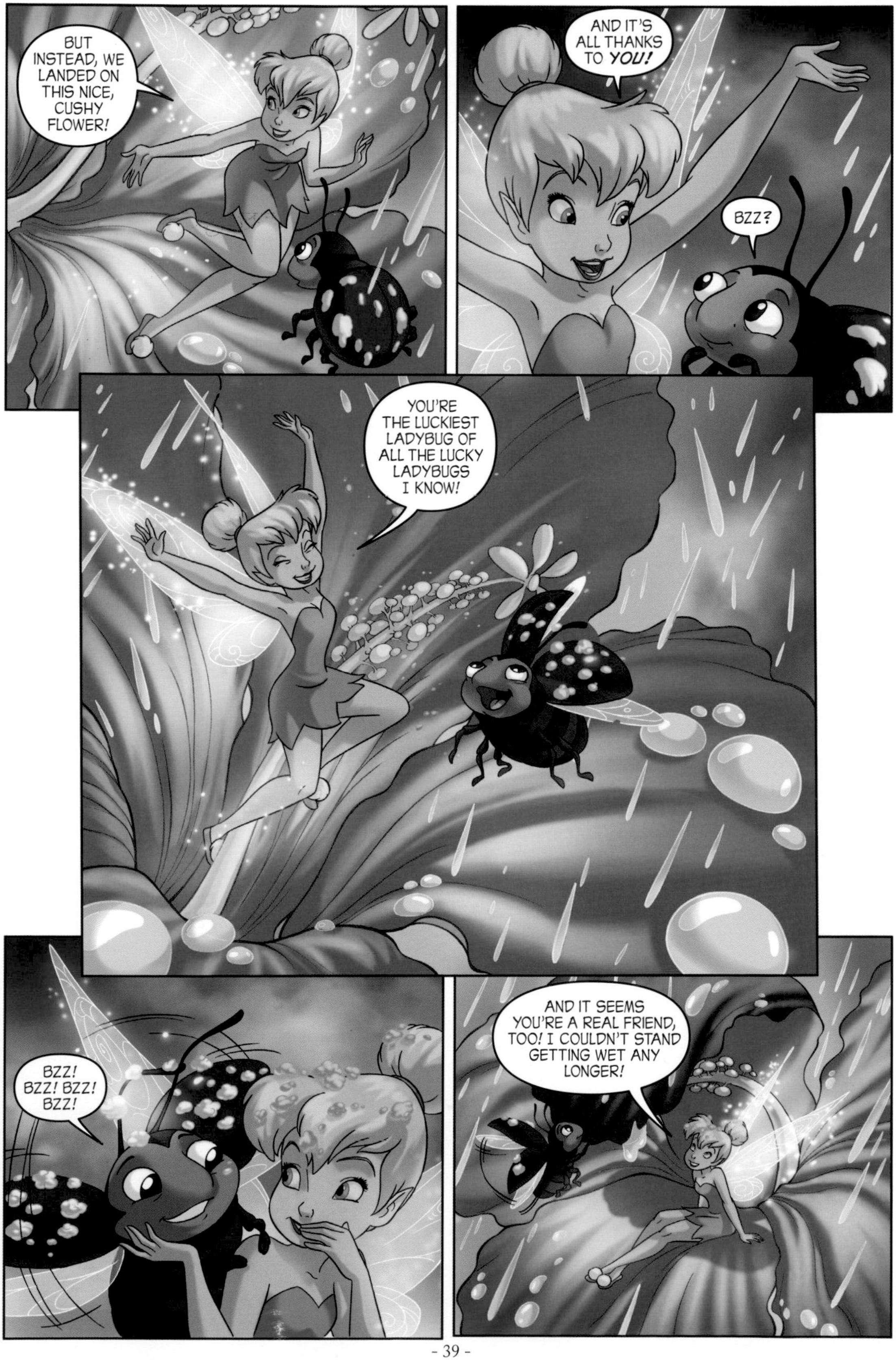
BUT INSTEAD, WE LANDED ON THIS NICE, CUSHY FLOWER!
AND IT'S ALL THANKS TO *YOU!*
BZZ?
YOU'RE THE LUCKIEST LADYBUG OF ALL THE LUCKY LADYBUGS I KNOW!
BZZ! BZZ! BZZ! BZZ!
AND IT SEEMS YOU'RE A REAL FRIEND, TOO! I COULDN'T STAND GETTING WET ANY LONGER!

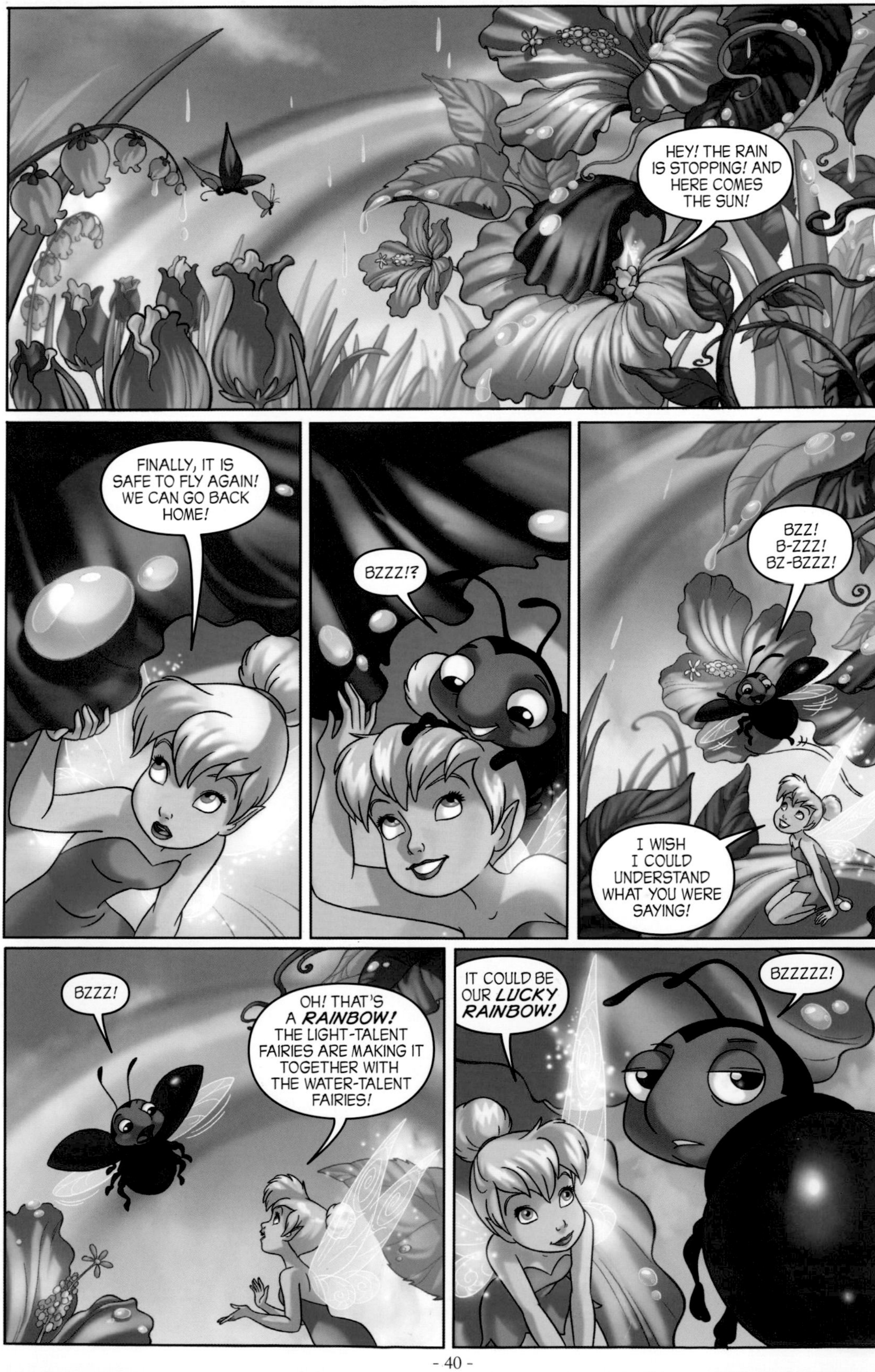
HEY! THE RAIN IS STOPPING! AND HERE COMES THE SUN!
FINALLY, IT IS SAFE TO FLY AGAIN! WE CAN GO BACK HOME!
BZZZ!?
BZZ! B-ZZZ! BZ-BZZZ!
I WISH I COULD UNDERSTAND WHAT YOU WERE SAYING!
BZZZ!
OH! THAT'S A ***RAINBOW!*** THE LIGHT-TALENT FAIRIES ARE MAKING IT TOGETHER WITH THE WATER-TALENT FAIRIES!
IT COULD BE OUR ***LUCKY RAINBOW!***
BZZZZZ!

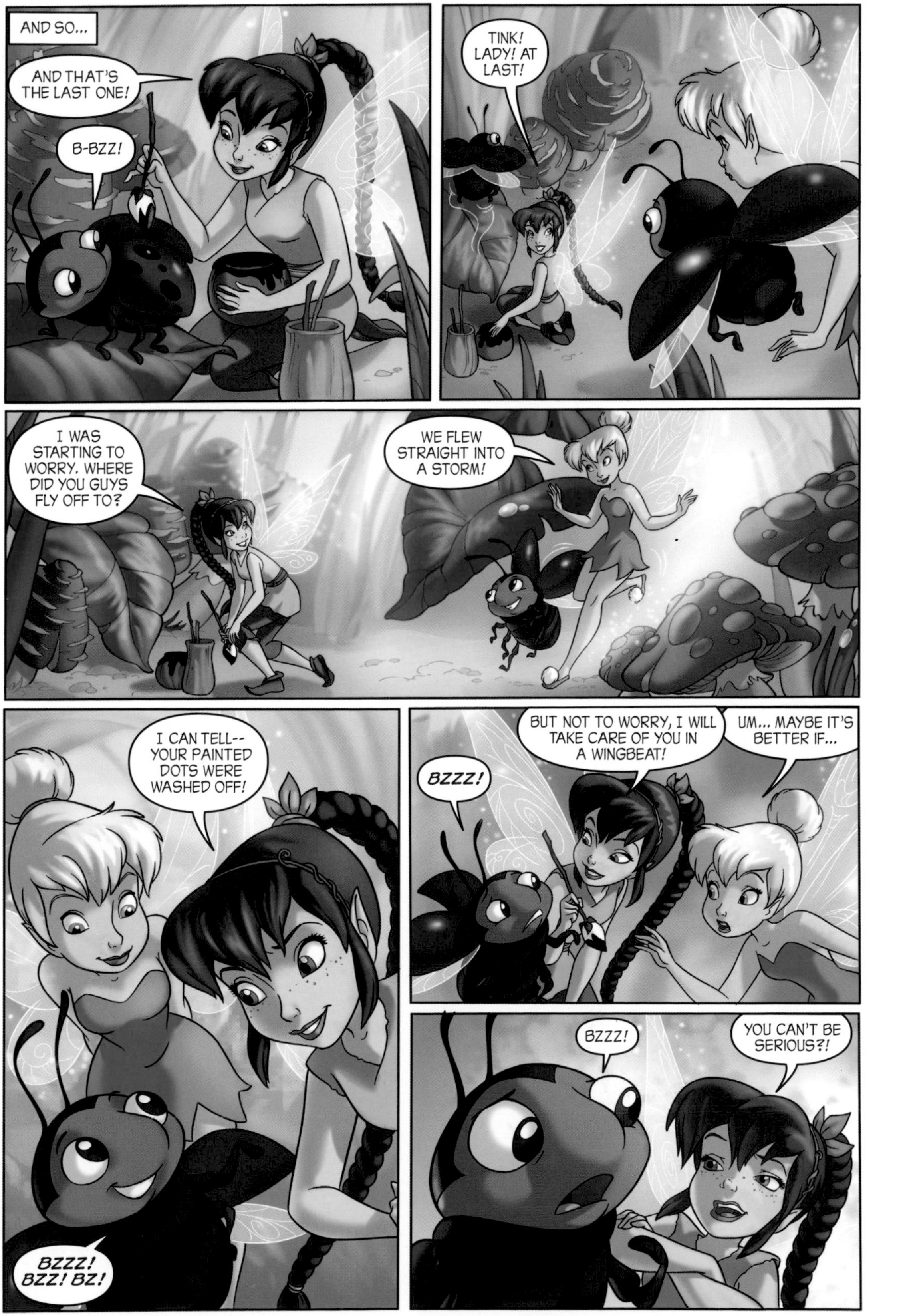
AND SO...
AND THAT'S THE LAST ONE!
B-BZZ!
TINK! LADY! AT LAST!
I WAS STARTING TO WORRY. WHERE DID YOU GUYS FLY OFF TO?
WE FLEW STRAIGHT INTO A STORM!
I CAN TELL-- YOUR PAINTED DOTS WERE WASHED OFF!
BZZZ! BZZ! BZ!
BZZZ!
BUT NOT TO WORRY, I WILL TAKE CARE OF YOU IN A WINGBEAT!
UM... MAYBE IT'S BETTER IF...
BZZZ!
YOU CAN'T BE SERIOUS?!

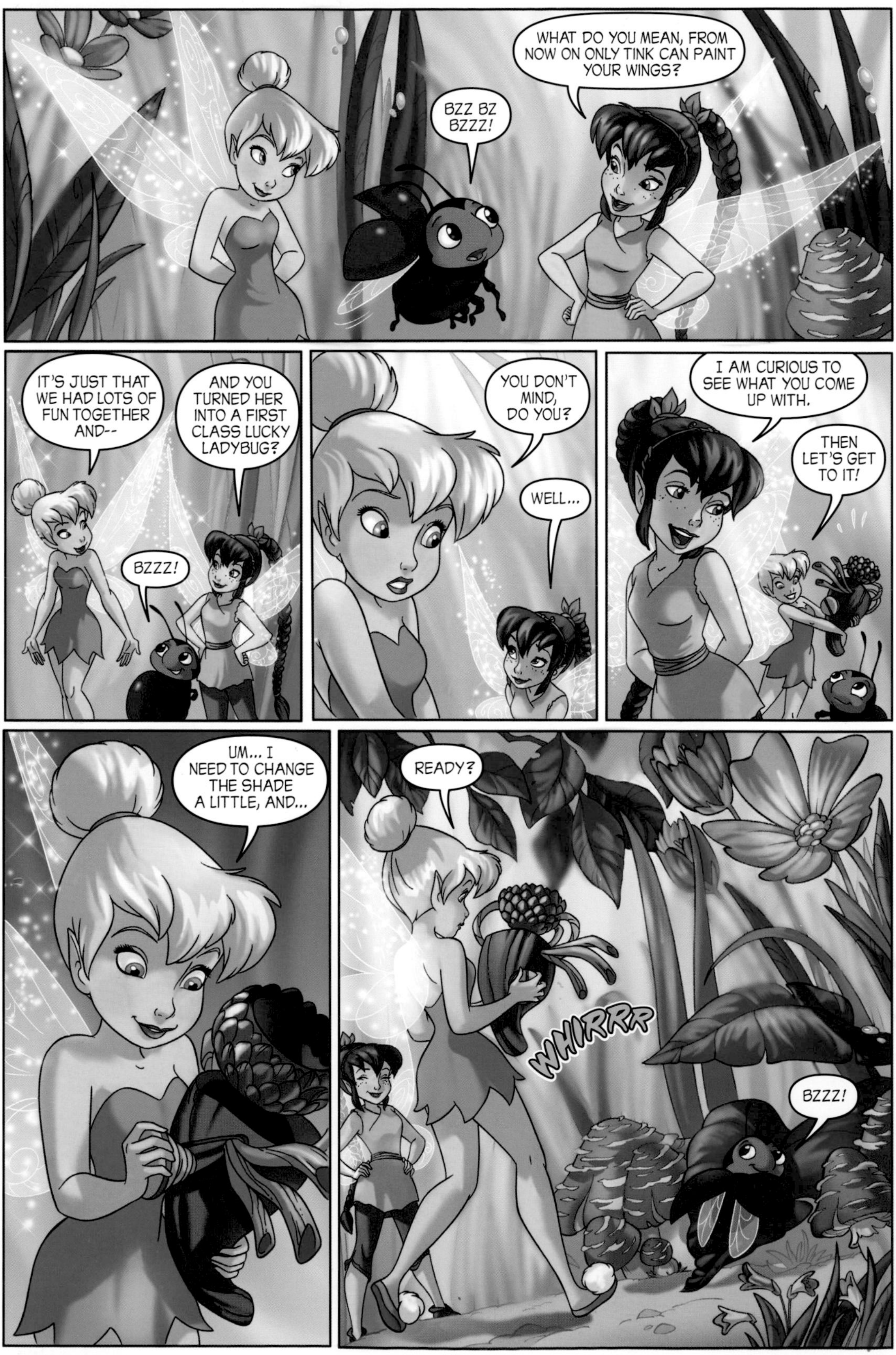
WHAT DO YOU MEAN, FROM NOW ON ONLY TINK CAN PAINT YOUR WINGS?
BZZ BZ BZZZ!
IT'S JUST THAT WE HAD LOTS OF FUN TOGETHER AND--
AND YOU TURNED HER INTO A FIRST CLASS LUCKY LADYBUG?
BZZZ!
YOU DON'T MIND, DO YOU?
WELL...
I AM CURIOUS TO SEE WHAT YOU COME UP WITH.
THEN LET'S GET TO IT!
UM... I NEED TO CHANGE THE SHADE A LITTLE, AND...
READY?
WHIRRR
BZZZ!

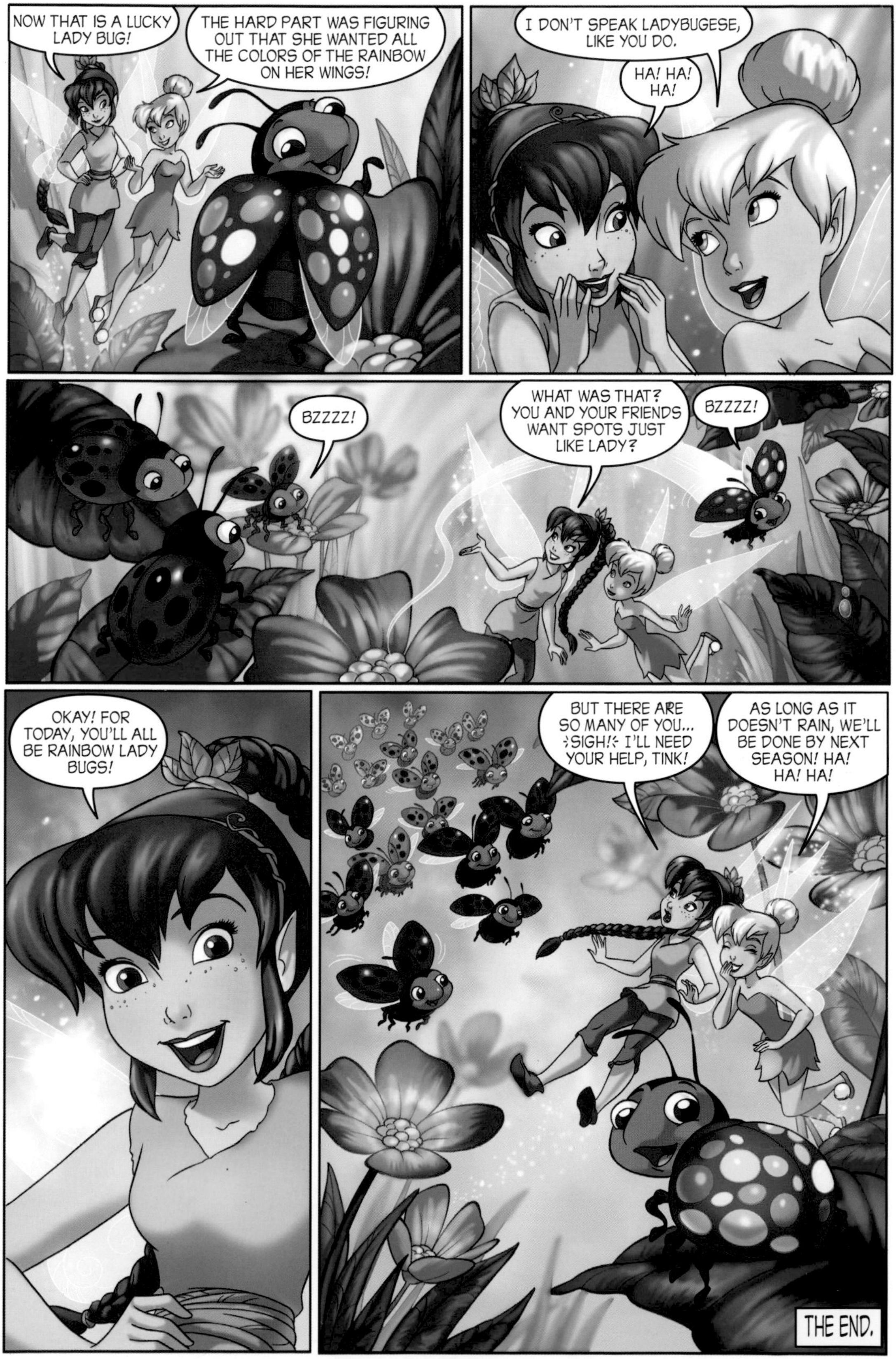
NOW THAT IS A LUCKY LADY BUG!
THE HARD PART WAS FIGURING OUT THAT SHE WANTED ALL THE COLORS OF THE RAINBOW ON HER WINGS!
I DON'T SPEAK LADYBUGESE, LIKE YOU DO.
HA! HA! HA!
BZZZZ!
WHAT WAS THAT? YOU AND YOUR FRIENDS WANT SPOTS JUST LIKE LADY?
BZZZZ!
OKAY! FOR TODAY, YOU'LL ALL BE RAINBOW LADY BUGS!
BUT THERE ARE SO MANY OF YOU... *SIGH!* I'LL NEED YOUR HELP, TINK!
AS LONG AS IT DOESN'T RAIN, WE'LL BE DONE BY NEXT SEASON! HA! HA! HA!
THE END.

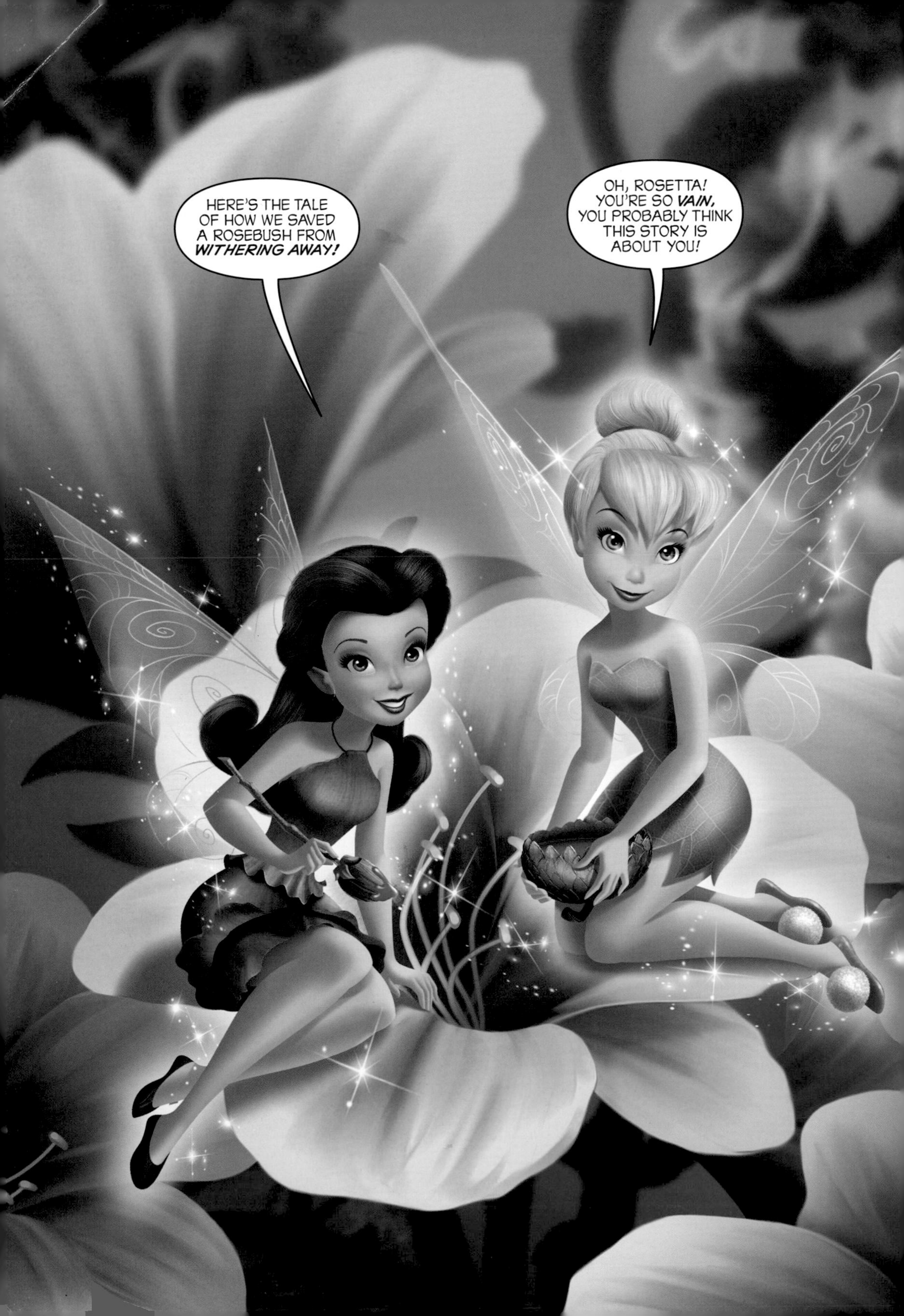
HERE'S THE TALE OF HOW WE SAVED A ROSEBUSH FROM WITHERING AWAY!
OH, ROSETTA! YOU'RE SO VAIN, YOU PROBABLY THINK THIS STORY IS ABOUT YOU!

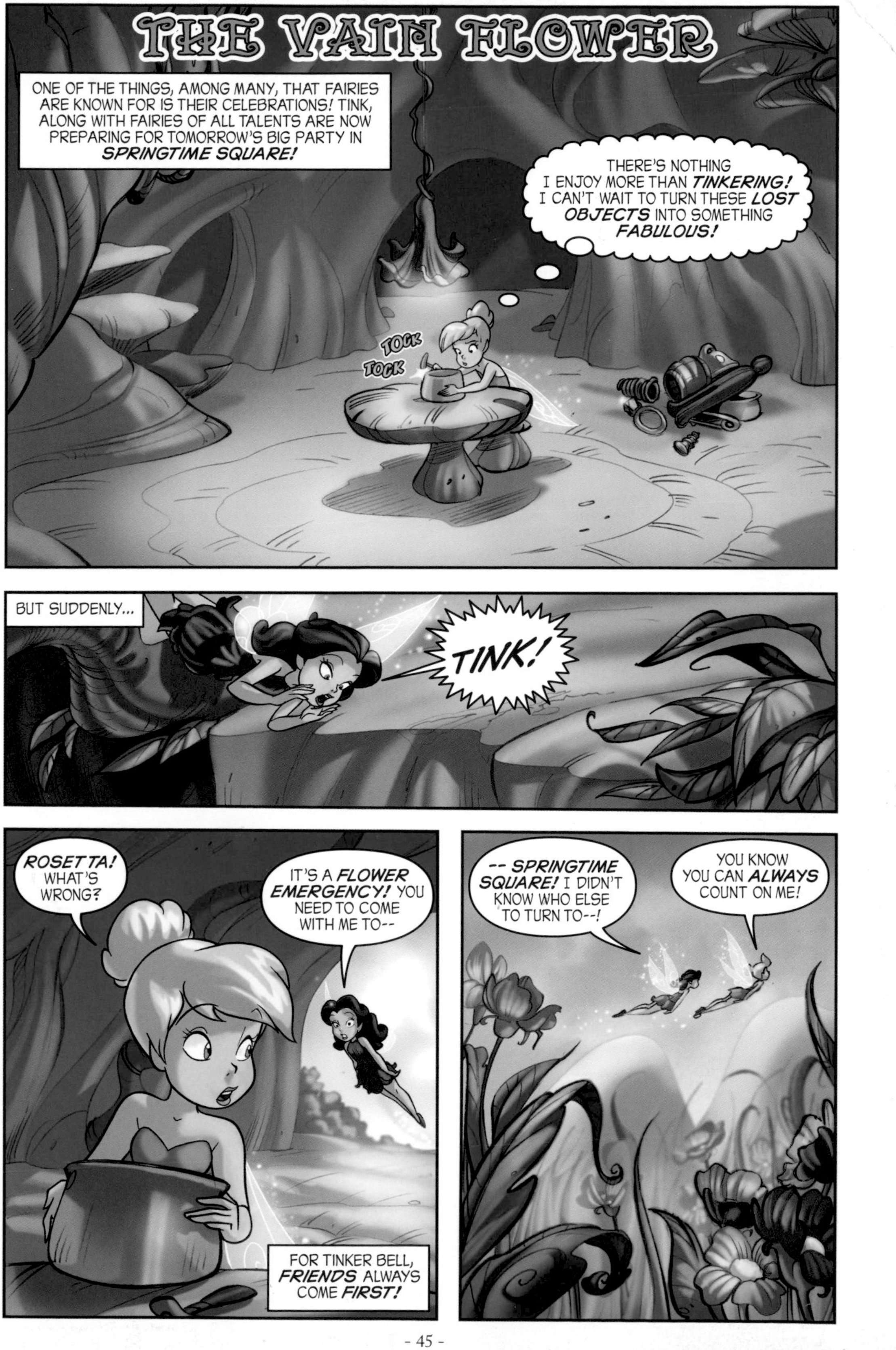
THE VAIN FLOWER
ONE OF THE THINGS, AMONG MANY, THAT FAIRIES ARE KNOWN FOR IS THEIR CELEBRATIONS! TINK, ALONG WITH FAIRIES OF ALL TALENTS ARE NOW PREPARING FOR TOMORROW'S BIG PARTY IN SPRINGTIME SQUARE!
THERE'S NOTHING I ENJOY MORE THAN TINKERING! I CAN'T WAIT TO TURN THESE LOST OBJECTS INTO SOMETHING FABULOUS!
TOCK
TOCK
BUT SUDDENLY...
TINK!
ROSETTA! WHAT'S WRONG?
IT'S A FLOWER EMERGENCY! YOU NEED TO COME WITH ME TO--
FOR TINKER BELL, FRIENDS ALWAYS COME FIRST!
-- SPRINGTIME SQUARE! I DIDN'T KNOW WHO ELSE TO TURN TO--!
YOU KNOW YOU CAN ALWAYS COUNT ON ME!

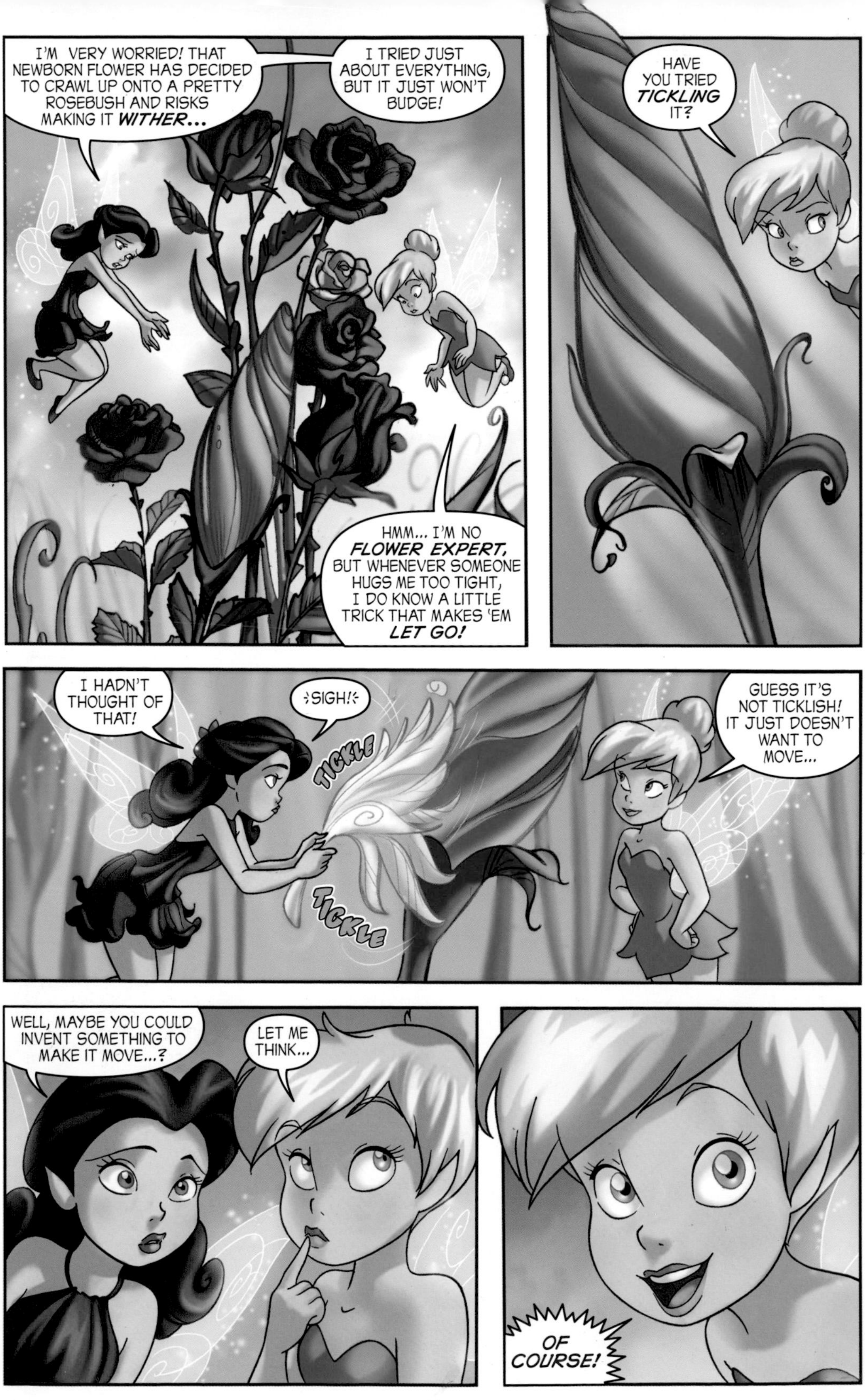

I'M VERY WORRIED! THAT NEWBORN FLOWER HAS DECIDED TO CRAWL UP ONTO A PRETTY ROSEBUSH AND RISKS MAKING IT WITHER...
I TRIED JUST ABOUT EVERYTHING, BUT IT JUST WON'T BUDGE!
HMM... I'M NO FLOWER EXPERT, BUT WHENEVER SOMEONE HUGS ME TOO TIGHT, I DO KNOW A LITTLE TRICK THAT MAKES 'EM LET GO!
HAVE YOU TRIED TICKLING IT?
I HADN'T THOUGHT OF THAT!
SIGH!
TICKLE
TICKLE
GUESS IT'S NOT TICKLISH! IT JUST DOESN'T WANT TO MOVE...
WELL, MAYBE YOU COULD INVENT SOMETHING TO MAKE IT MOVE...?
LET ME THINK...
OF COURSE!

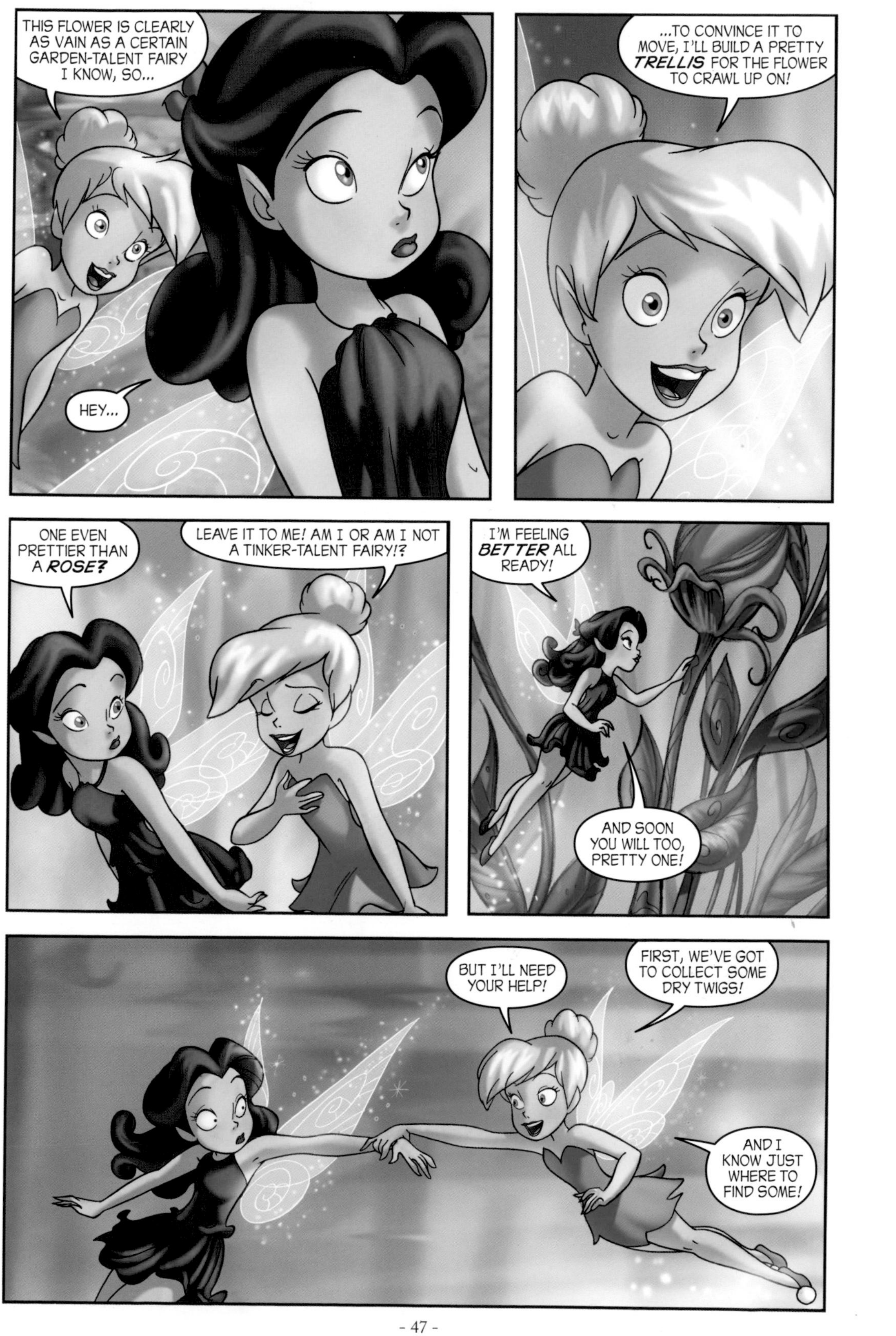

THIS FLOWER IS CLEARLY AS VAIN AS A CERTAIN GARDEN-TALENT FAIRY I KNOW, SO...
HEY...
...TO CONVINCE IT TO MOVE, I'LL BUILD A PRETTY TRELLIS FOR THE FLOWER TO CRAWL UP ON!
ONE EVEN PRETTIER THAN A ROSE?
LEAVE IT TO ME! AM I OR AM I NOT A TINKER-TALENT FAIRY!?
I'M FEELING BETTER ALL READY!
AND SOON YOU WILL TOO, PRETTY ONE!
BUT I'LL NEED YOUR HELP!
FIRST, WE'VE GOT TO COLLECT SOME DRY TWIGS!
AND I KNOW JUST WHERE TO FIND SOME!

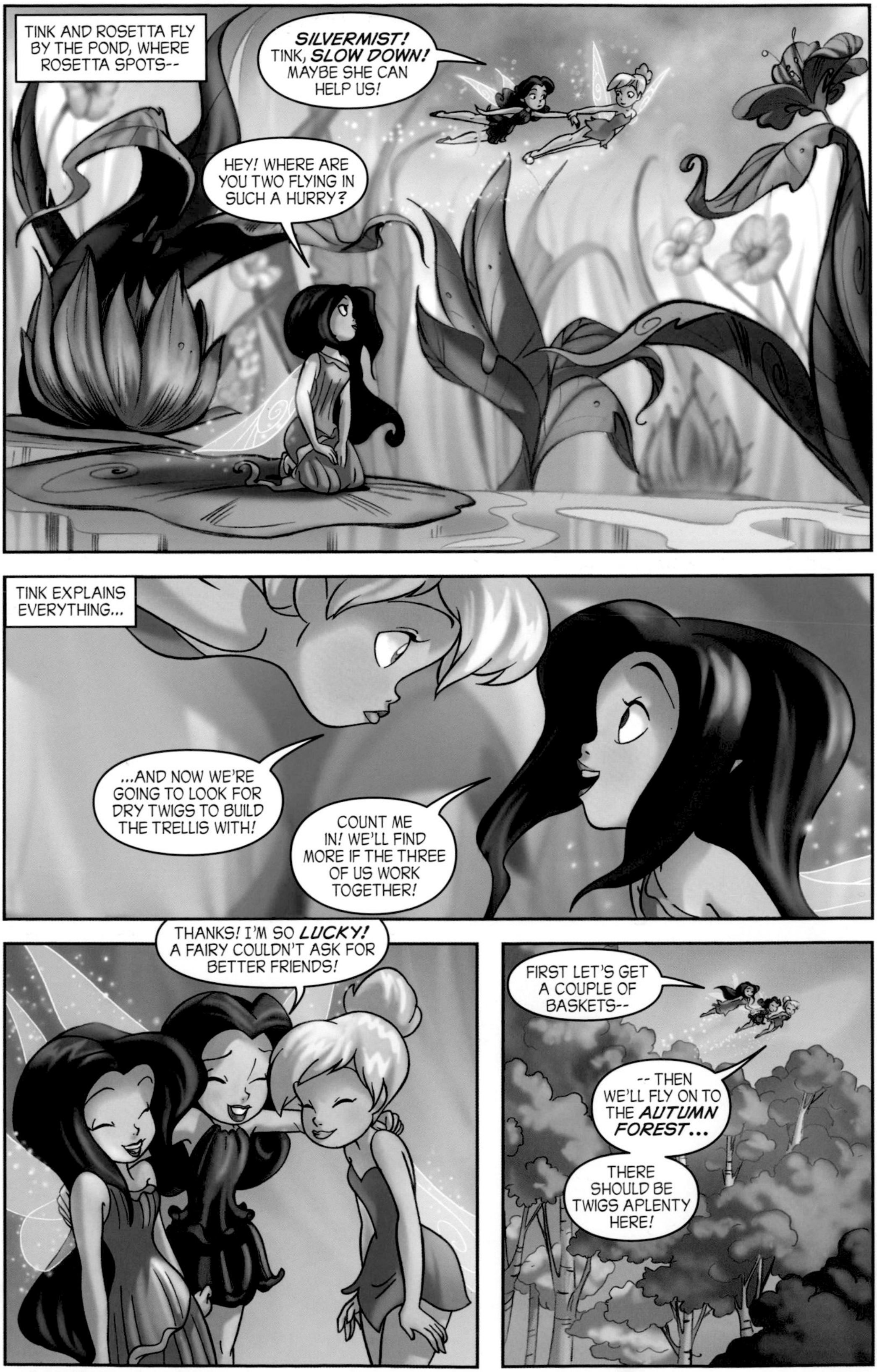
TINK AND ROSETTA FLY BY THE POND, WHERE ROSETTA SPOTS--
SILVERMIST! TINK, SLOW DOWN! MAYBE SHE CAN HELP US!
HEY! WHERE ARE YOU TWO FLYING IN SUCH A HURRY?
TINK EXPLAINS EVERYTHING...
...AND NOW WE'RE GOING TO LOOK FOR DRY TWIGS TO BUILD THE TRELLIS WITH!
COUNT ME IN! WE'LL FIND MORE IF THE THREE OF US WORK TOGETHER!
THANKS! I'M SO LUCKY! A FAIRY COULDN'T ASK FOR BETTER FRIENDS!
FIRST LET'S GET A COUPLE OF BASKETS--
-- THEN WE'LL FLY ON TO THE AUTUMN FOREST...
THERE SHOULD BE TWIGS APLENTY HERE!

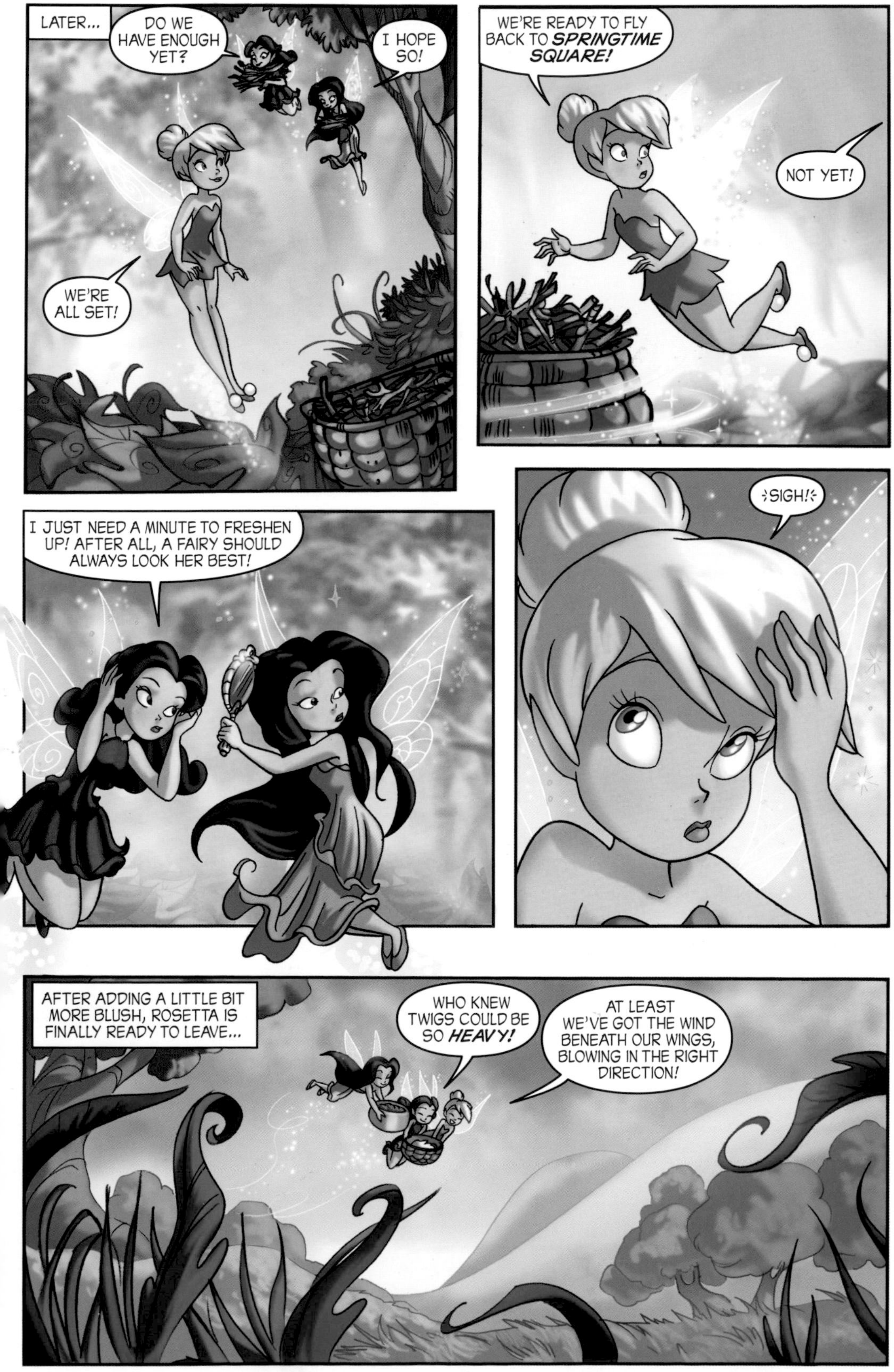
LATER...
DO WE HAVE ENOUGH YET?
I HOPE SO!
WE'RE ALL SET!
WE'RE READY TO FLY BACK TO SPRINGTIME SQUARE!
NOT YET!
I JUST NEED A MINUTE TO FRESHEN UP! AFTER ALL, A FAIRY SHOULD ALWAYS LOOK HER BEST!
SIGH!
AFTER ADDING A LITTLE BIT MORE BLUSH, ROSETTA IS FINALLY READY TO LEAVE...
WHO KNEW TWIGS COULD BE SO HEAVY!
AT LEAST WE'VE GOT THE WIND BENEATH OUR WINGS, BLOWING IN THE RIGHT DIRECTION!

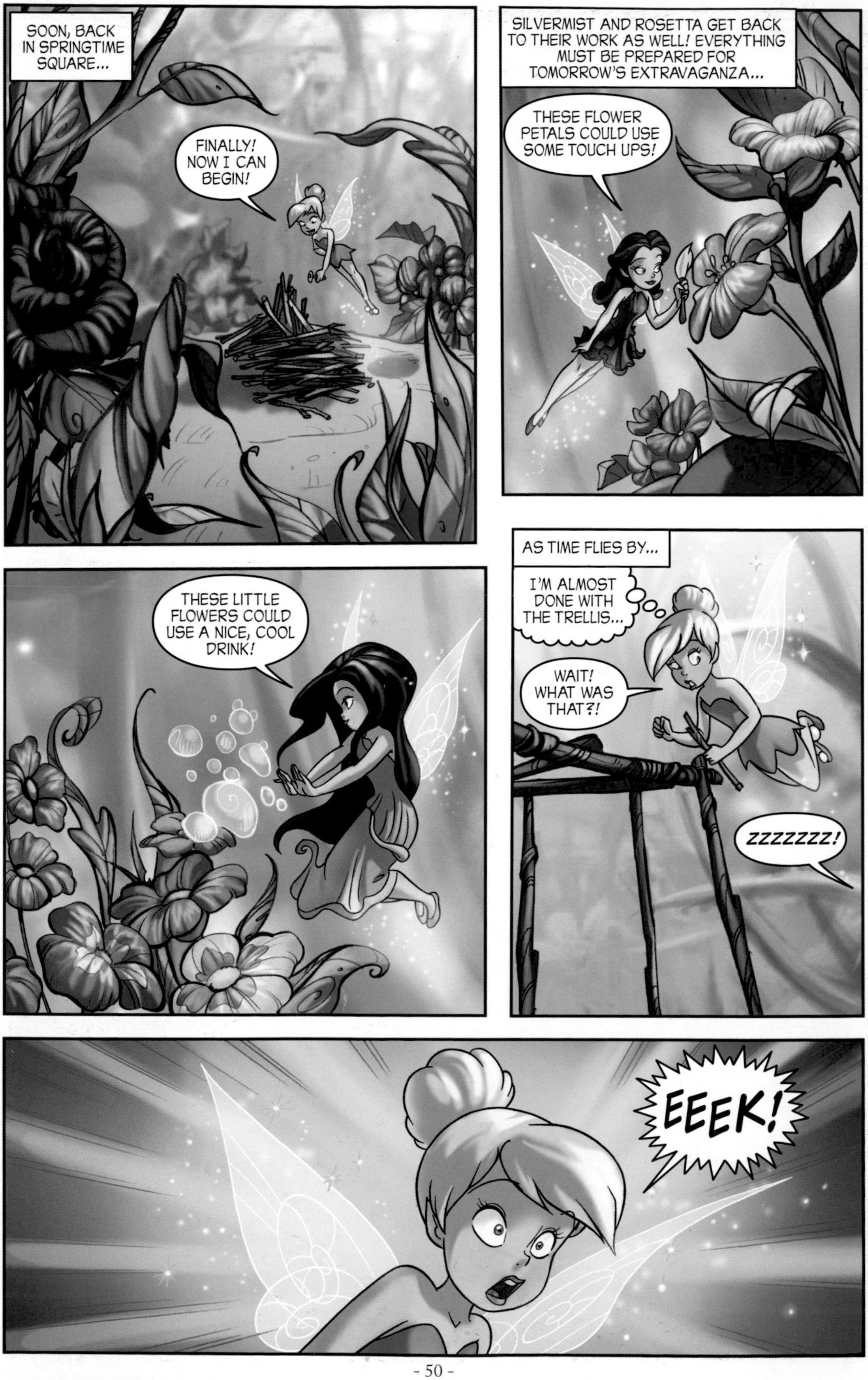
SOON, BACK IN SPRINGTIME SQUARE...
FINALLY! NOW I CAN BEGIN!
SILVERMIST AND ROSETTA GET BACK TO THEIR WORK AS WELL! EVERYTHING MUST BE PREPARED FOR TOMORROW'S EXTRAVAGANZA...
THESE FLOWER PETALS COULD USE SOME TOUCH UPS!
THESE LITTLE FLOWERS COULD USE A NICE, COOL DRINK!
AS TIME FLIES BY...
I'M ALMOST DONE WITH THE TRELLIS...
WAIT! WHAT WAS THAT?!
ZZZZZZZ!
EEEK!

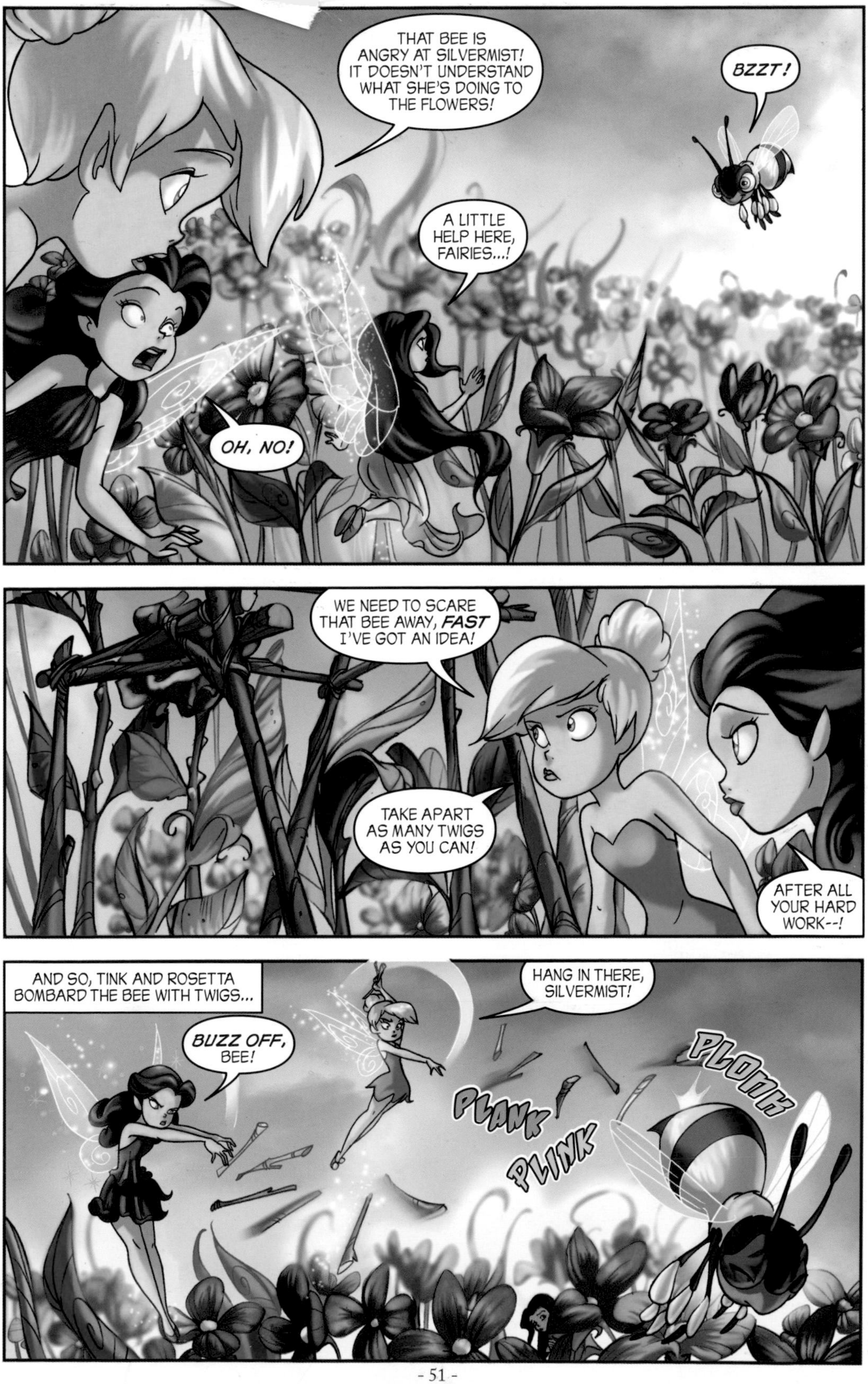
THAT BEE IS ANGRY AT SILVERMIST! IT DOESN'T UNDERSTAND WHAT SHE'S DOING TO THE FLOWERS!
BZZT!
A LITTLE HELP HERE, FAIRIES...!
OH, NO!
WE NEED TO SCARE THAT BEE AWAY, FAST I'VE GOT AN IDEA!
TAKE APART AS MANY TWIGS AS YOU CAN!
AFTER ALL YOUR HARD WORK--!
AND SO, TINK AND ROSETTA BOMBARD THE BEE WITH TWIGS...
HANG IN THERE, SILVERMIST!
BUZZ OFF, BEE!
PLANK
PLINK
PLONK

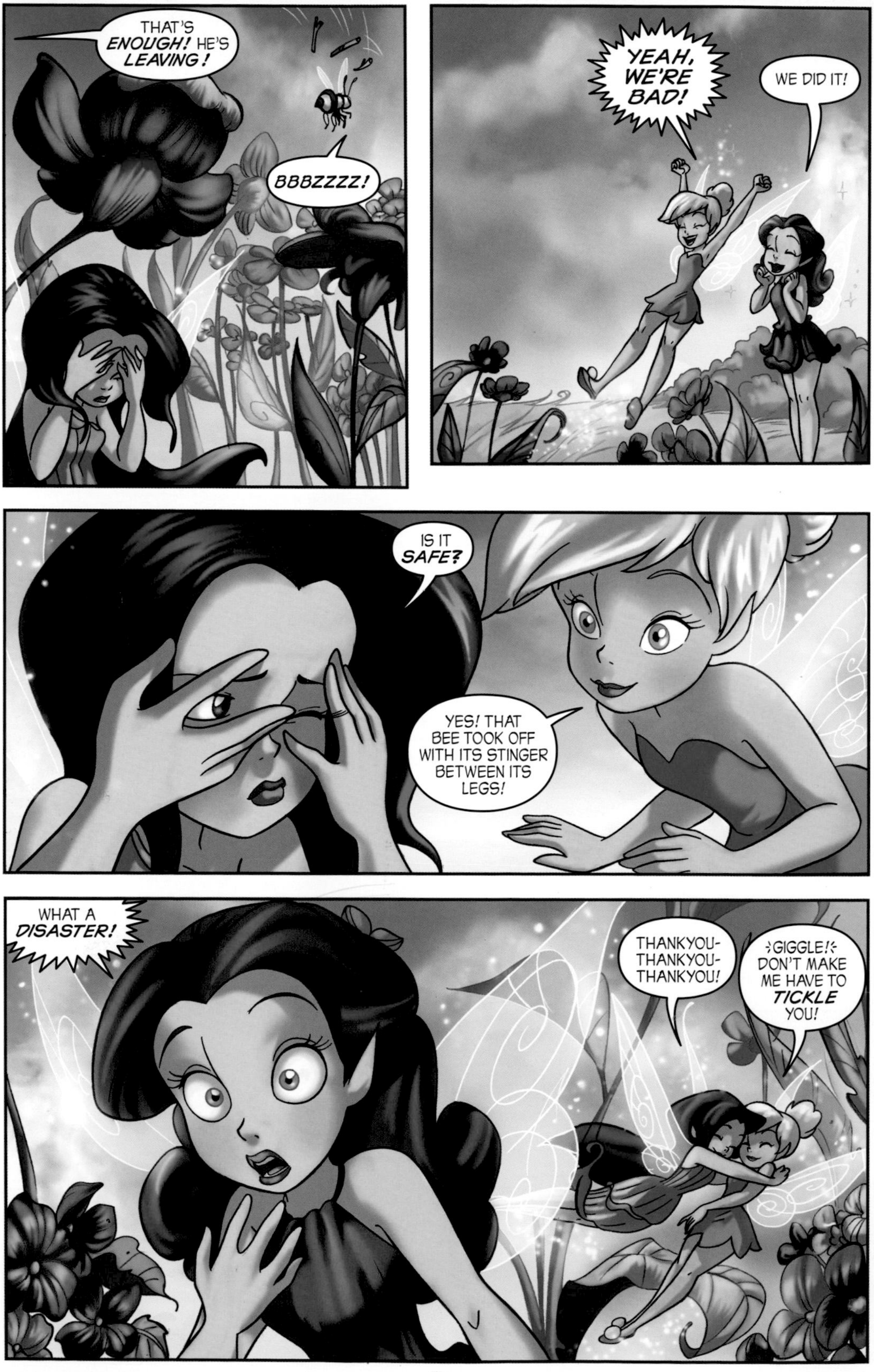
THAT'S ENOUGH! HE'S LEAVING!
BBBZZZZ!
YEAH, WE'RE BAD!
WE DID IT!
IS IT SAFE?
YES! THAT BEE TOOK OFF WITH ITS STINGER BETWEEN ITS LEGS!
WHAT A DISASTER!
THANKYOU-THANKYOU-THANKYOU!
GIGGLE! DON'T MAKE ME HAVE TO TICKLE YOU!

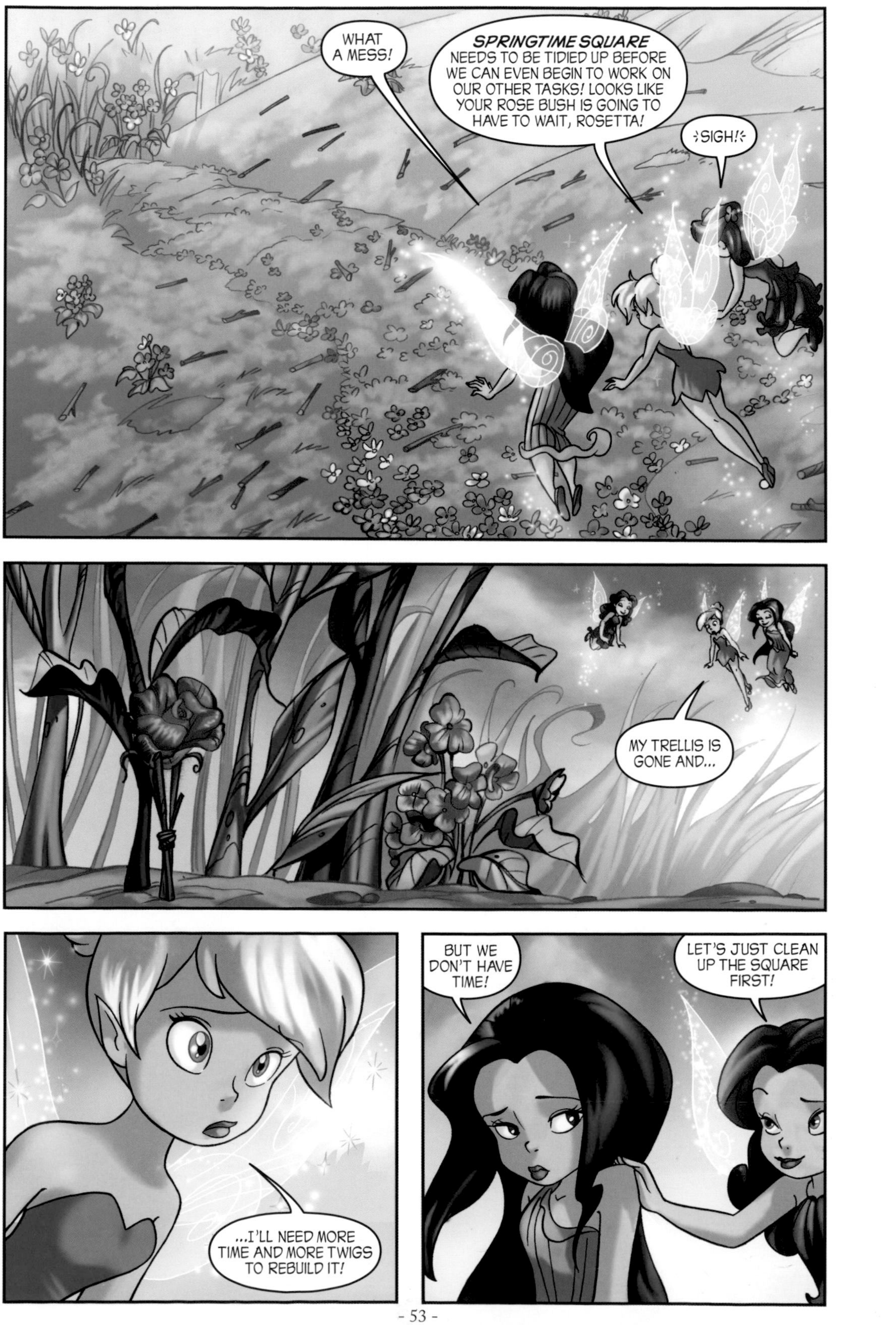
WHAT A MESS!
SPRINGTIME SQUARE NEEDS TO BE TIDIED UP BEFORE WE CAN EVEN BEGIN TO WORK ON OUR OTHER TASKS! LOOKS LIKE YOUR ROSE BUSH IS GOING TO HAVE TO WAIT, ROSETTA!
SIGH!
MY TRELLIS IS GONE AND...
...I'LL NEED MORE TIME AND MORE TWIGS TO REBUILD IT!
BUT WE DON'T HAVE TIME!
LET'S JUST CLEAN UP THE SQUARE FIRST!

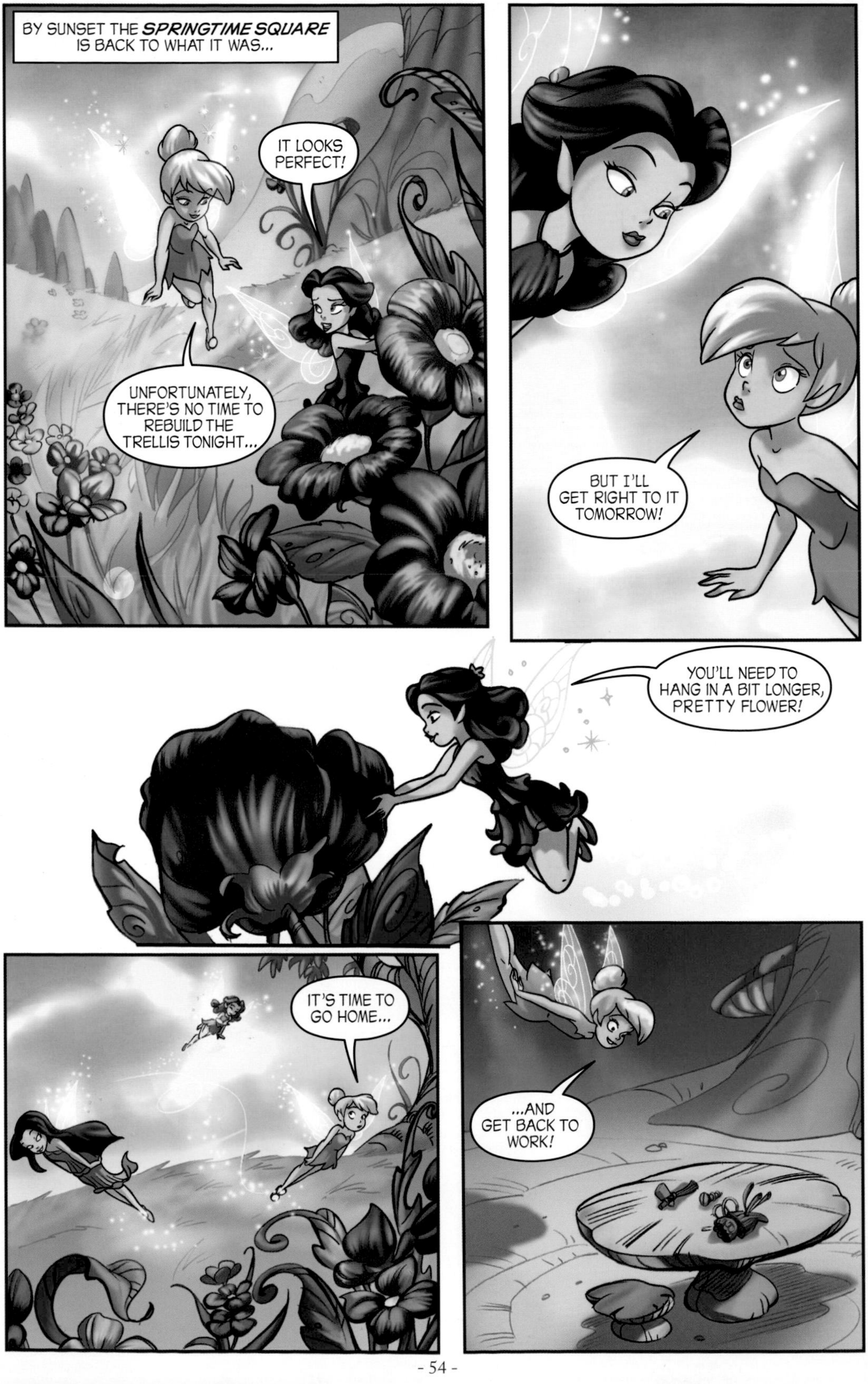
BY SUNSET THE SPRINGTIME SQUARE IS BACK TO WHAT IT WAS...
IT LOOKS PERFECT!
UNFORTUNATELY, THERE'S NO TIME TO REBUILD THE TRELLIS TONIGHT...
BUT I'LL GET RIGHT TO IT TOMORROW!
YOU'LL NEED TO HANG IN A BIT LONGER, PRETTY FLOWER!
IT'S TIME TO GO HOME...
...AND GET BACK TO WORK!

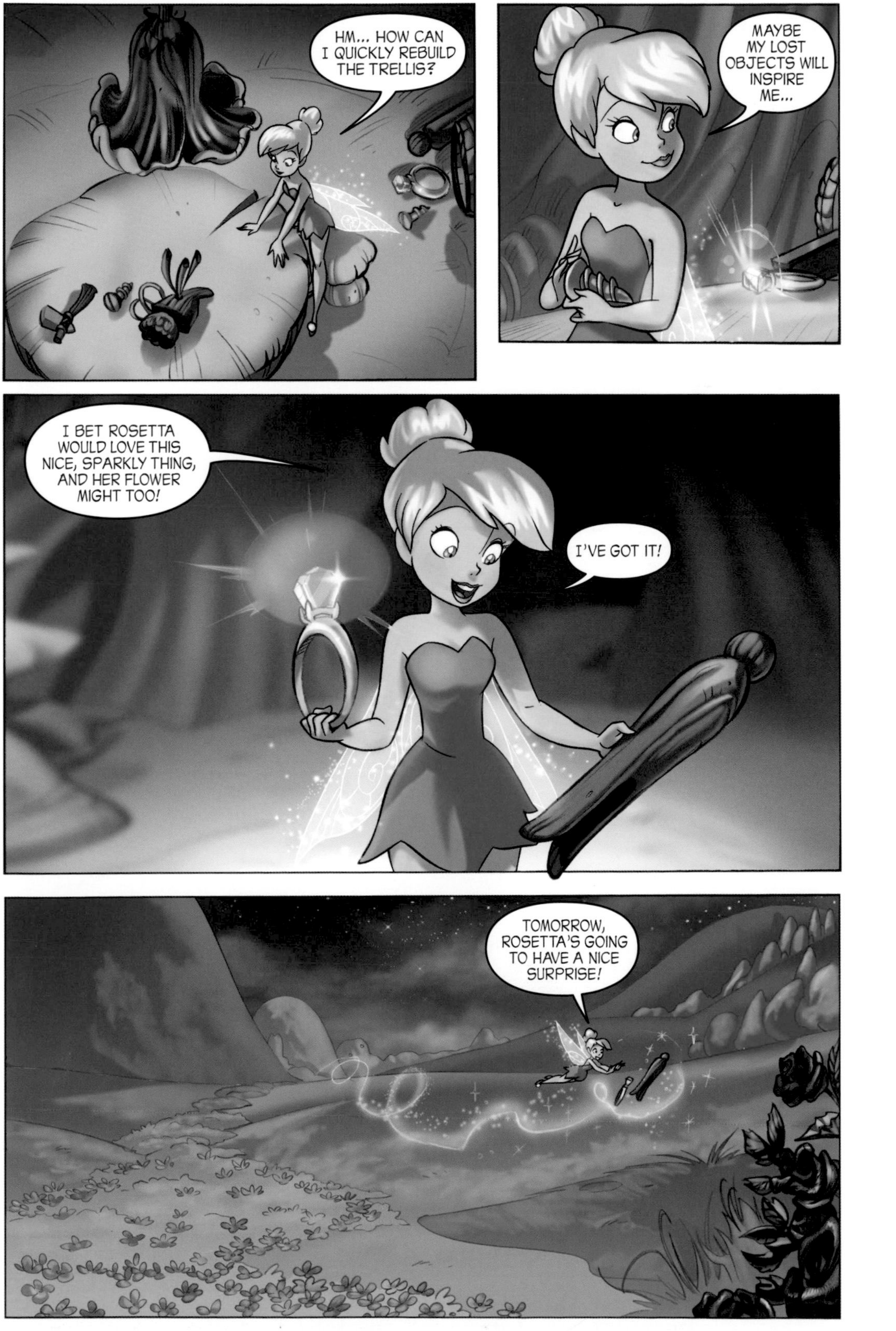
HM... HOW CAN I QUICKLY REBUILD THE TRELLIS?
MAYBE MY LOST OBJECTS WILL INSPIRE ME...
I BET ROSETTA WOULD LOVE THIS NICE, SPARKLY THING, AND HER FLOWER MIGHT TOO!
I'VE GOT IT!
TOMORROW, ROSETTA'S GOING TO HAVE A NICE SURPRISE!

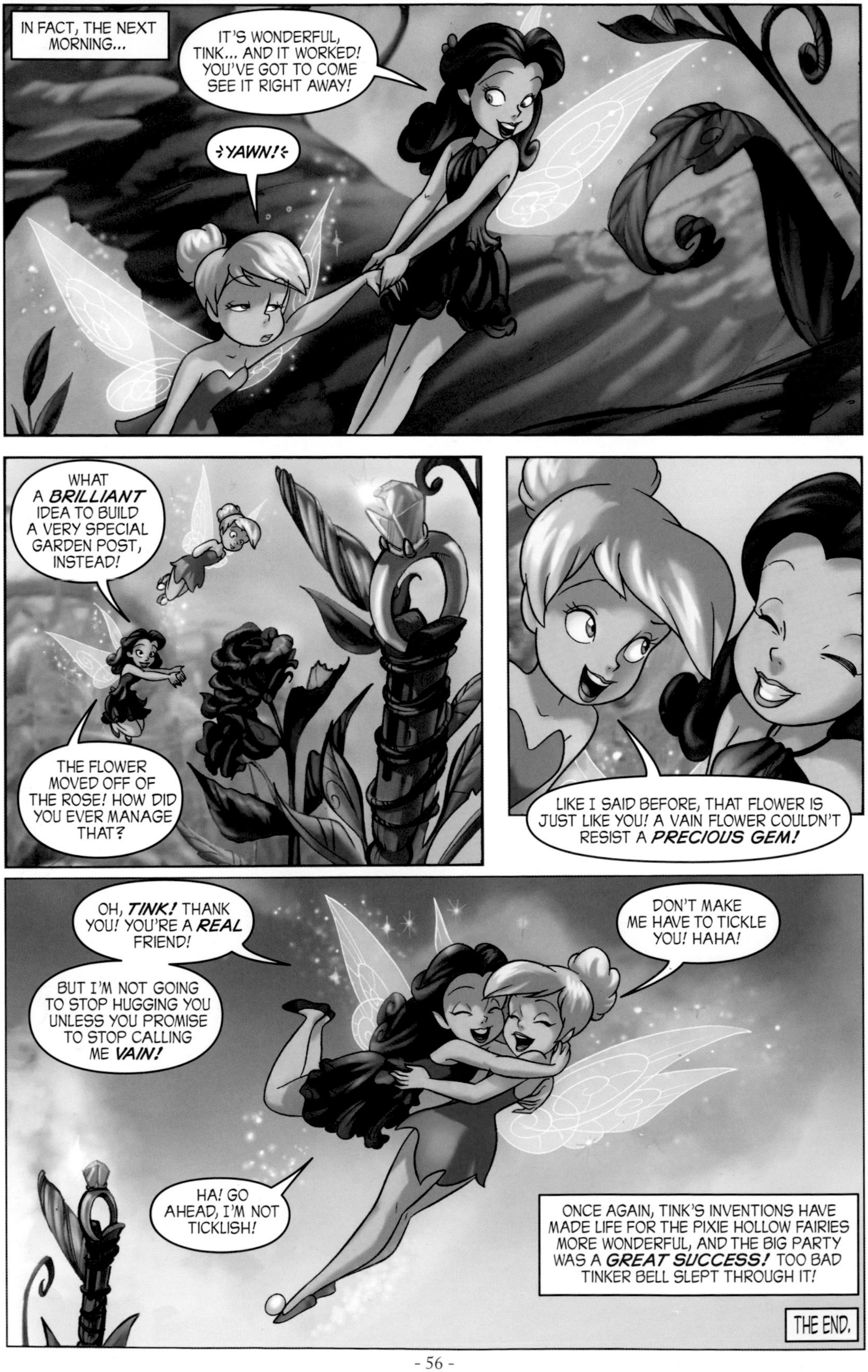
IN FACT, THE NEXT MORNING...
IT'S WONDERFUL, TINK... AND IT WORKED! YOU'VE GOT TO COME SEE IT RIGHT AWAY!
YAWN!
WHAT A BRILLIANT IDEA TO BUILD A VERY SPECIAL GARDEN POST, INSTEAD!
THE FLOWER MOVED OFF OF THE ROSE! HOW DID YOU EVER MANAGE THAT?
LIKE I SAID BEFORE, THAT FLOWER IS JUST LIKE YOU! A VAIN FLOWER COULDN'T RESIST A PRECIOUS GEM!
OH, TINK! THANK YOU! YOU'RE A REAL FRIEND!
BUT I'M NOT GOING TO STOP HUGGING YOU UNLESS YOU PROMISE TO STOP CALLING ME VAIN!
DON'T MAKE ME HAVE TO TICKLE YOU! HAHA!
HA! GO AHEAD, I'M NOT TICKLISH!
ONCE AGAIN, TINK'S INVENTIONS HAVE MADE LIFE FOR THE PIXIE HOLLOW FAIRIES MORE WONDERFUL, AND THE BIG PARTY WAS A GREAT SUCCESS! TOO BAD TINKER BELL SLEPT THROUGH IT!
THE END.

WATCH OUT FOR PAPERCUTZ™

Welcome to the tenth (technically the eleventh, if you count TINKER BELL AND THE GREAT FAIRY RESCUE), tender-hearted DISNEY FAIRIES graphic novel from Papercutz, those pixies dedicated to magically creating great graphic novels for all ages! I'm Jim Salicrup, the Editor-in-Chief and part-time pretend pirate. ARRR.

When I was just a child, one of my dreams was to work in comics. I didn't know then that I'd wind up being an editor, as most people have no idea exactly what a comicbook editor does, and I didn't have a clue back then either. I probably hoped to become a comicbook artist, as I loved drawing, and I just loved the artwork found in all my favorite comics. It was great fun to study the artwork and discover the subtle differences in various artists' styles, as no two artists tend to draw exactly alike.

We've been super-fortunate to have many amazing artists in the pages of DISNEY FAIRIES, each one offering their own magical take on Tinker Bell and her friends. The first artist of this illustrious group whose work I've been able to identify is Antonello Dalena. You can see two great examples of his layout artistry in "The Enchanted Gem" and "The Vain Flower" in this volume of DISNEY FAIRIES. The reason I'm able to spot his work is that we're also publishing two other graphic novel series illustrated by the prolific Mr. Dalena at Papercutz: SYBIL and ERNEST & REBECCA. So, to help you become more familiar with Antonello's work, here's a little checklist of previous stories he's drawn in DISNEY FAIRIES:

In DISNEY FAIRIES #7 "Tinker Bell the Perfect Fairy" Antonello, working with Manuela Razzi, penciled "No Need for Words" and "Tink, the Perfect Fairy." In DISNEY FAIRIES #9 "Tinker Bell and her Magical Arrival" Antonello penciled all four stories based on the hit DVD, "The Magical Arrival," "A New Talent,""The Magic in You," and "A Fairy May be Near."

On the following pages we thought you might enjoy seeing a few pages from ERNEST & REBECCA #3 "Grandpa Bug," about a six-and-a-half year old girl, and her best friend, who is a microbe named Ernest. Following that, we've got a special preview of DISNEY FAIRIES #11 "Tinker Bell and the Most Precious Gift."

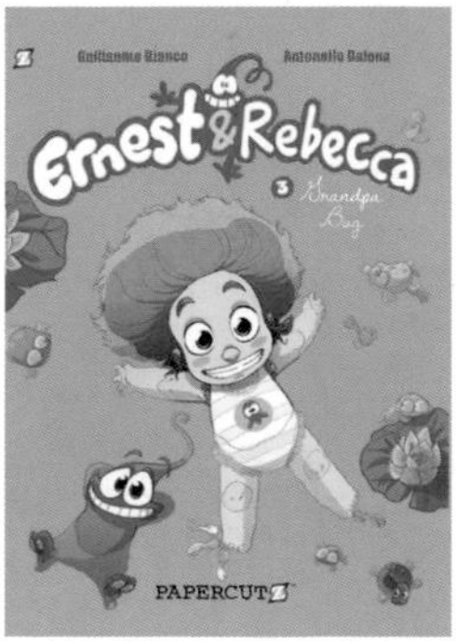
Antonello Dalena
Ernest & Rebecca
3 Grandpa Bug
PAPERCUTZ

So, while I didn't grow up to be a fantastic artist like Antonello Dalena, I did get to become an editor who gets to enjoy his work, and all the other great artists published by Papercutz. So, if you want your dreams to come true too, remember to keep believing in "faith, trust, and pixie dust"!

Jim

STAY IN TOUCH!

EMAIL:	salicrup@papercutz.com
WEB:	www.papercutz.com
TWITTER:	@papercutzgn
FACEBOOK:	PAPERCUTZGRAPHICNOVELS
REGULAR MAIL:	Papercutz, 160 Broadway, Suite 700, East Wing, New York, NY 10038

Special Preview of ERNEST & REBECCA #3 "Grandpa Bug"...

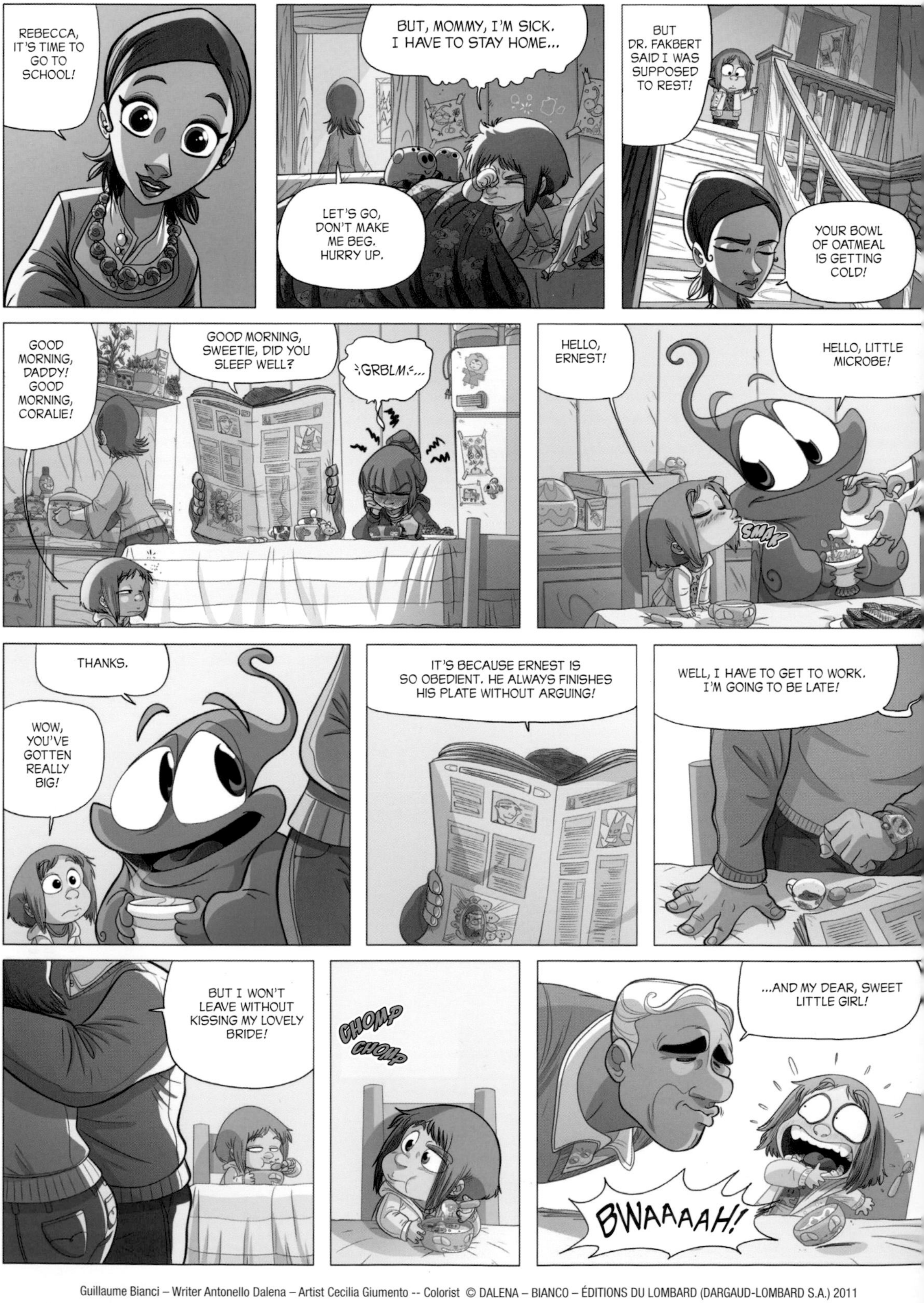
REBECCA, IT'S TIME TO GO TO SCHOOL!
BUT, MOMMY, I'M SICK. I HAVE TO STAY HOME...
LET'S GO, DON'T MAKE ME BEG. HURRY UP.
BUT DR. FAKBERT SAID I WAS SUPPOSED TO REST!
YOUR BOWL OF OATMEAL IS GETTING COLD!
GOOD MORNING, DADDY! GOOD MORNING, CORALIE!
GOOD MORNING, SWEETIE, DID YOU SLEEP WELL?
GRBLM...
HELLO, ERNEST!
HELLO, LITTLE MICROBE!
SMAK
THANKS.
WOW, YOU'VE GOTTEN REALLY BIG!
IT'S BECAUSE ERNEST IS SO OBEDIENT. HE ALWAYS FINISHES HIS PLATE WITHOUT ARGUING!
WELL, I HAVE TO GET TO WORK. I'M GOING TO BE LATE!
BUT I WON'T LEAVE WITHOUT KISSING MY LOVELY BRIDE!
CHOMP
CHOMP
...AND MY DEAR, SWEET LITTLE GIRL!
BWAAAAH!

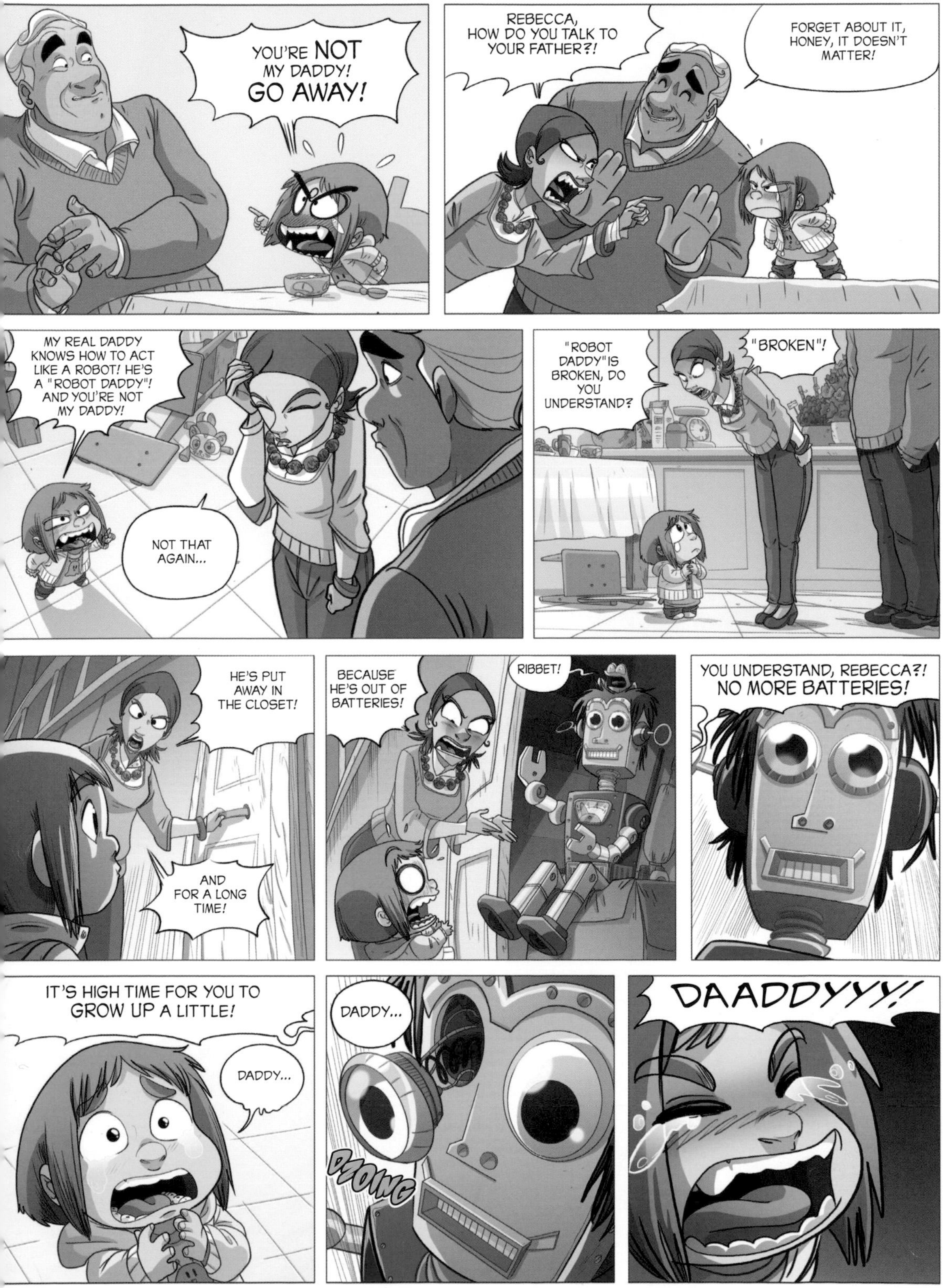

YOU'RE NOT MY DADDY! GO AWAY!
REBECCA, HOW DO YOU TALK TO YOUR FATHER?!
FORGET ABOUT IT, HONEY, IT DOESN'T MATTER!
MY REAL DADDY KNOWS HOW TO ACT LIKE A ROBOT! HE'S A "ROBOT DADDY"! AND YOU'RE NOT MY DADDY!
NOT THAT AGAIN...
"ROBOT DADDY" IS BROKEN, DO YOU UNDERSTAND?
"BROKEN"!
HE'S PUT AWAY IN THE CLOSET!
AND FOR A LONG TIME!
BECAUSE HE'S OUT OF BATTERIES!
RIBBET!
YOU UNDERSTAND, REBECCA?! NO MORE BATTERIES!
IT'S HIGH TIME FOR YOU TO GROW UP A LITTLE!
DADDY...
DADDY...
DZOING
DAADDYYY!

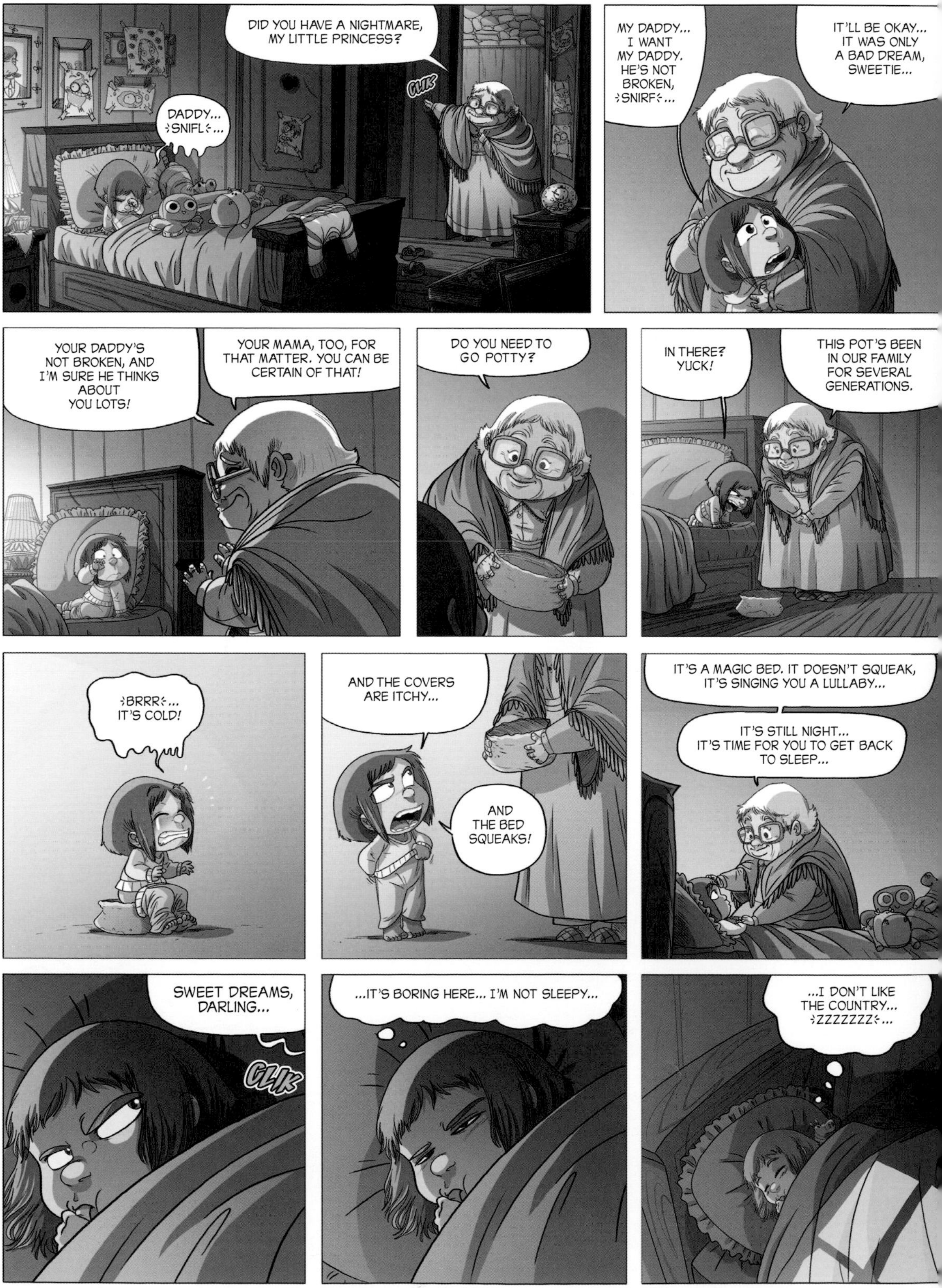
DID YOU HAVE A NIGHTMARE, MY LITTLE PRINCESS?
CLIK
DADDY... ⟡SNIFL⟡...
MY DADDY... I WANT MY DADDY. HE'S NOT BROKEN, ⟡SNIRF⟡...
IT'LL BE OKAY... IT WAS ONLY A BAD DREAM, SWEETIE...
YOUR DADDY'S NOT BROKEN, AND I'M SURE HE THINKS ABOUT YOU LOTS!
YOUR MAMA, TOO, FOR THAT MATTER. YOU CAN BE CERTAIN OF THAT!
DO YOU NEED TO GO POTTY?
IN THERE? YUCK!
THIS POT'S BEEN IN OUR FAMILY FOR SEVERAL GENERATIONS.
⟡BRRR⟡... IT'S COLD!
AND THE COVERS ARE ITCHY...
AND THE BED SQUEAKS!
IT'S A MAGIC BED. IT DOESN'T SQUEAK, IT'S SINGING YOU A LULLABY...
IT'S STILL NIGHT... IT'S TIME FOR YOU TO GET BACK TO SLEEP...
SWEET DREAMS, DARLING...
CLIK
...IT'S BORING HERE... I'M NOT SLEEPY...
...I DON'T LIKE THE COUNTRY... ⟡ZZZZZZZ⟡...

Special Preview of DISNEY FAIRIES #11 "Tinker Bell and the Most Precious Gift"...

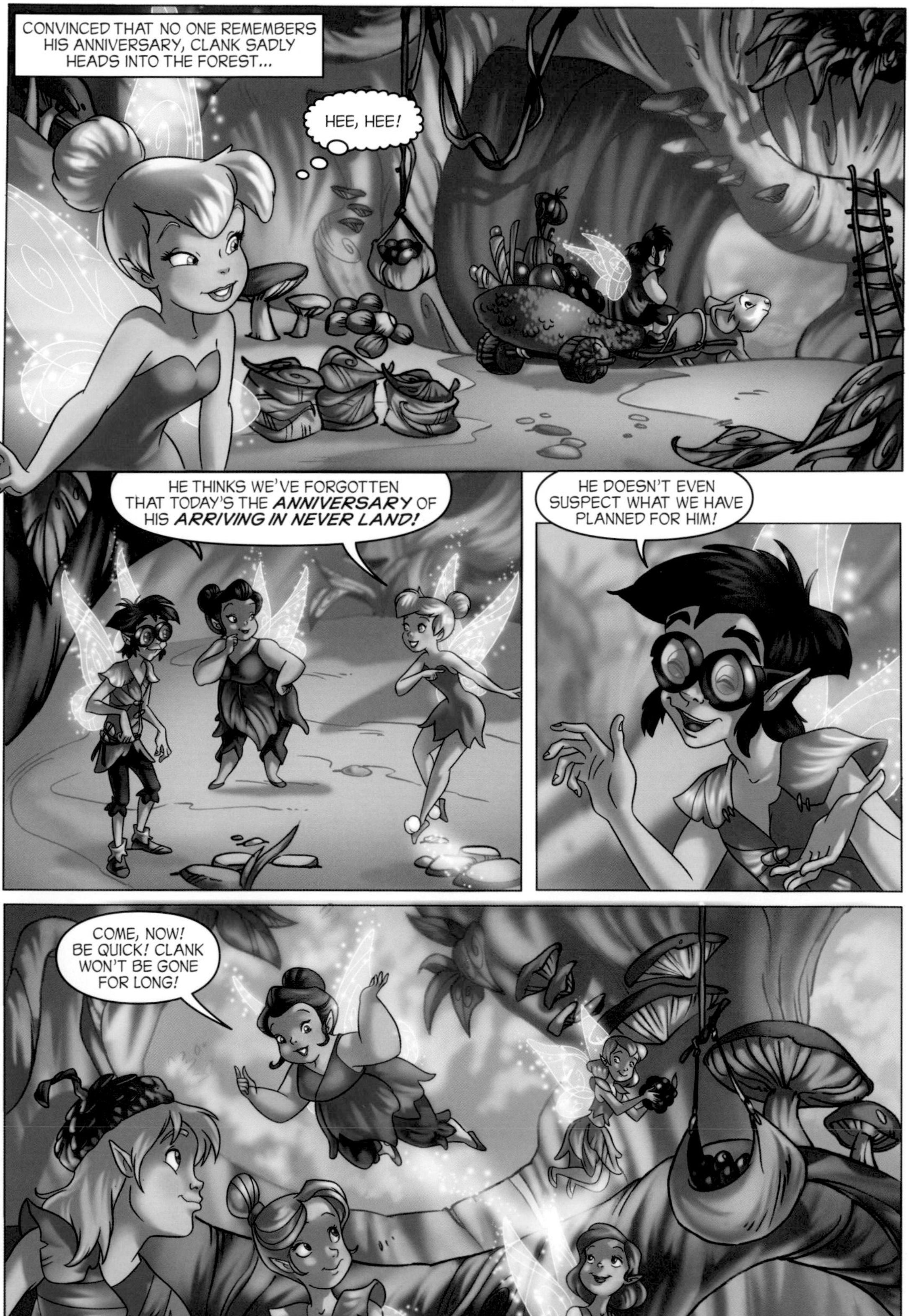
CONVINCED THAT NO ONE REMEMBERS HIS ANNIVERSARY, CLANK SADLY HEADS INTO THE FOREST...
HEE, HEE!
HE THINKS WE'VE FORGOTTEN THAT TODAY'S THE ANNIVERSARY OF HIS ARRIVING IN NEVER LAND!
HE DOESN'T EVEN SUSPECT WHAT WE HAVE PLANNED FOR HIM!
COME, NOW! BE QUICK! CLANK WON'T BE GONE FOR LONG!

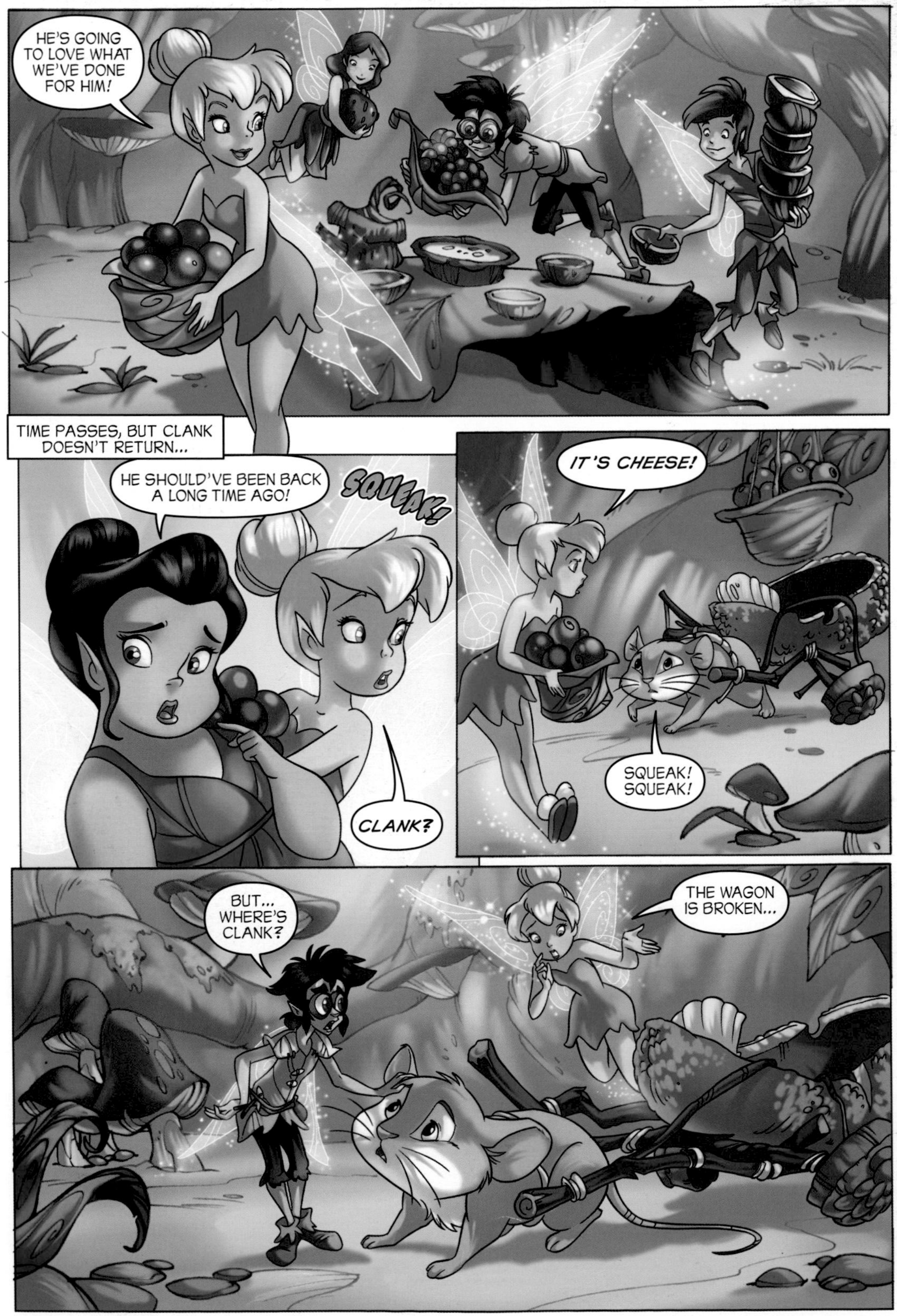
HE'S GOING TO LOVE WHAT WE'VE DONE FOR HIM!
TIME PASSES, BUT CLANK DOESN'T RETURN...
HE SHOULD'VE BEEN BACK A LONG TIME AGO!
SQUEAK!
CLANK?
IT'S CHEESE!
SQUEAK! SQUEAK!
BUT... WHERE'S CLANK?
THE WAGON IS BROKEN...

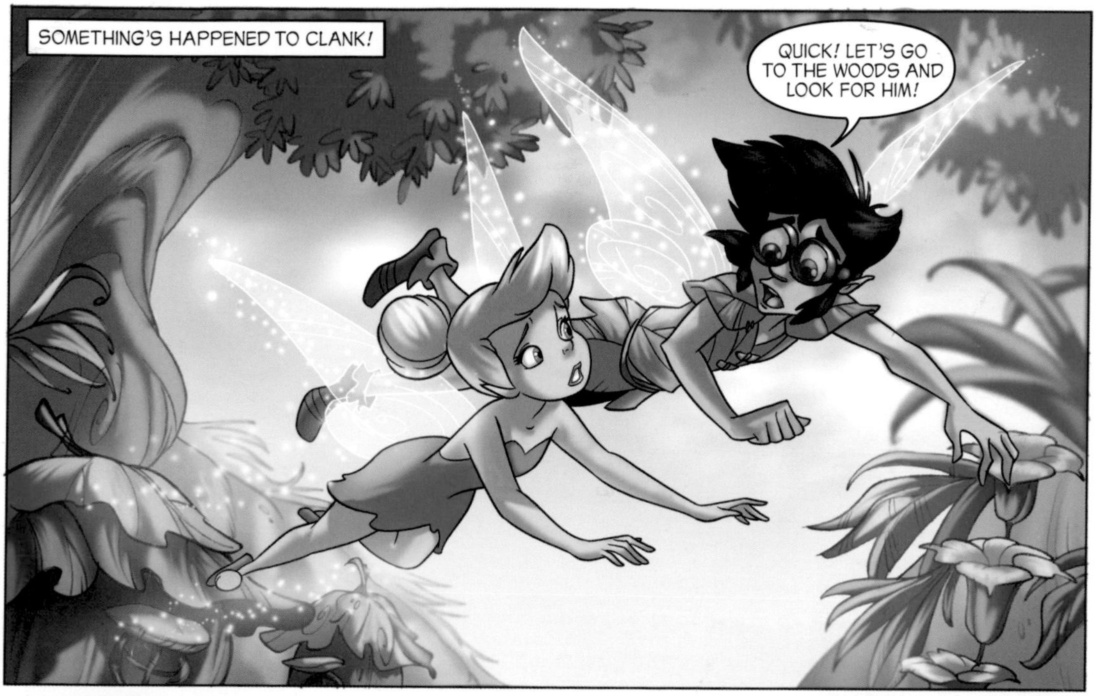
SOMETHING'S HAPPENED TO CLANK!
QUICK! LET'S GO TO THE WOODS AND LOOK FOR HIM!

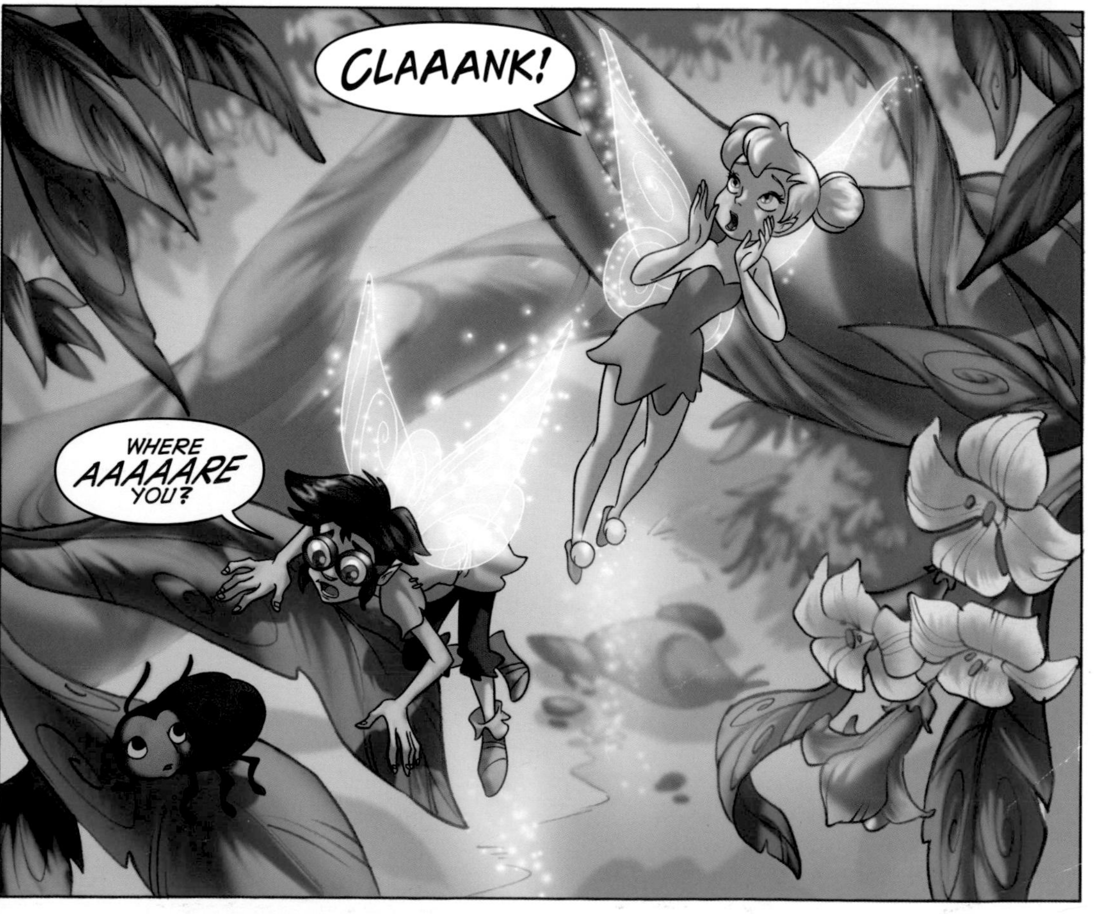
CLAAANK!
WHERE AAAAARE YOU?

Don't miss DISNEY FAIRIES #11 "Tinker Bell and the Most Precious Gift"!

More Great Graphic Novels from PAPERCUTZ™

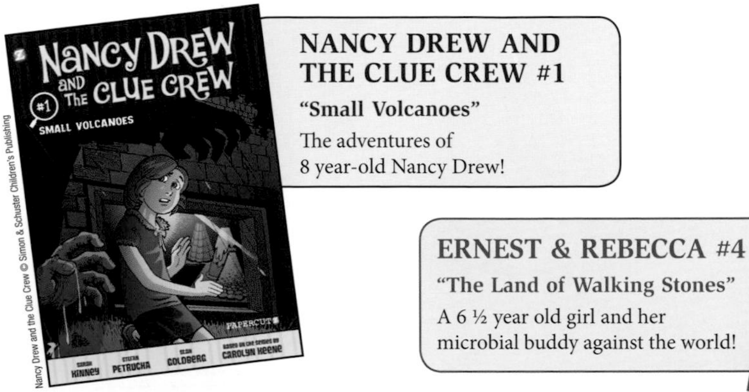

Nancy Drew and the Clue Crew
#1
SMALL VOLCANOES
PAPERCUTZ
SARAH KINNEY
STEFAN PETRUCHA
SEAN GOLDBERG
BASED ON THE SERIES BY CAROLYN KEENE

NANCY DREW AND THE CLUE CREW #1
"Small Volcanoes"
The adventures of
8 year-old Nancy Drew!

ERNEST & REBECCA #4
"The Land of Walking Stones"
A 6 ½ year old girl and her
microbial buddy against the world!

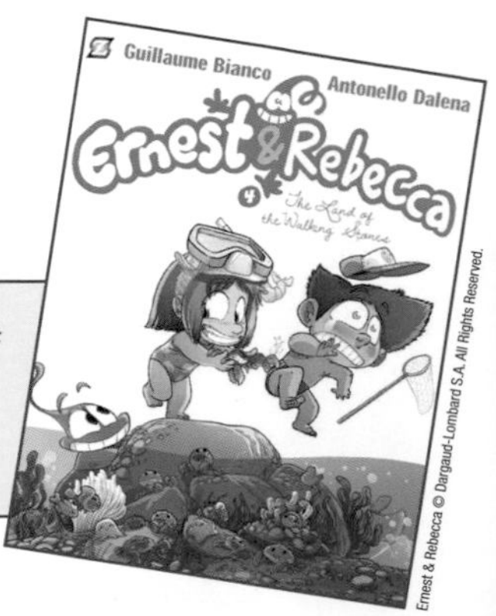

Guillaume Bianco
Antonello Dalena
Ernest & Rebecca

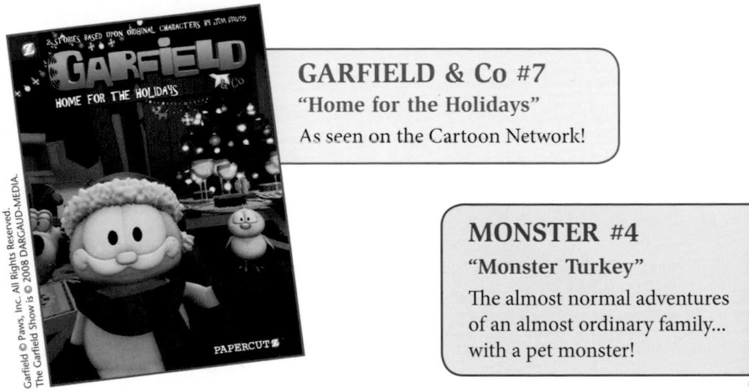

GARFIELD
& Co
HOME FOR THE HOLIDAYS
PAPERCUTZ

GARFIELD & Co #7
"Home for the Holidays"
As seen on the Cartoon Network!

MONSTER #4
"Monster Turkey"
The almost normal adventures
of an almost ordinary family...
with a pet monster!

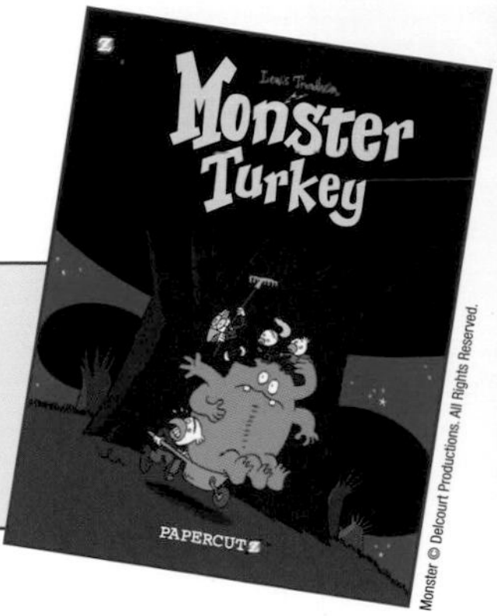

Monster Turkey
PAPERCUTZ

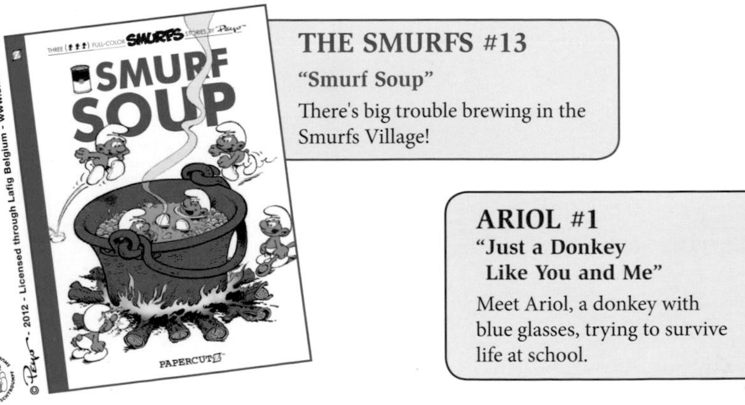

SMURFS
SMURF SOUP
PAPERCUTZ

THE SMURFS #13
"Smurf Soup"
There's big trouble brewing in the
Smurfs Village!

ARIOL #1
**"Just a Donkey
Like You and Me"**
Meet Ariol, a donkey with
blue glasses, trying to survive
life at school.

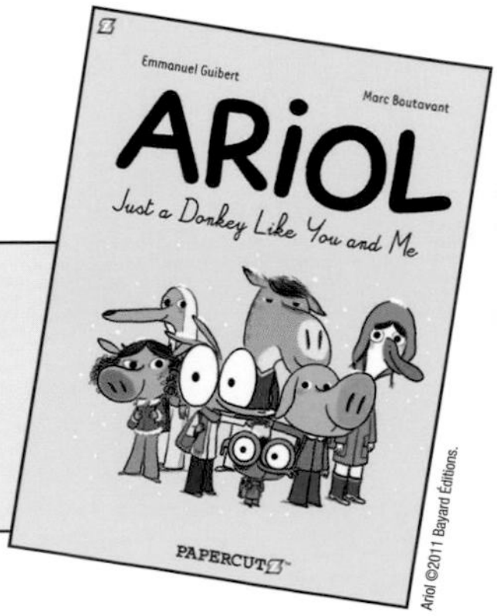

Emmanuel Guibert
Marc Boutavant
ARiOL
Just a Donkey Like You and Me
PAPERCUTZ

Available at better booksellers everywhere!

Or order directly from us! NANCY DREW AND THE CLUE CREW is available in paperback for $6.99, in hardcover for $10.99; ERNEST & REBECCA is $11.99 in hardcover only; GARFIELD & Co is available in hardcover only for $7.99; MONSTER is available in hardcover only for $9.99; THE SMURFS are available in paperback for $5.99, in hardcover for $10.99; ARIOL is available in paperback only for $12.99.

Please add $4.00 for postage and handling for the first book, add $1.00 for each additional book.

Please make check payable to NBM Publishing. Send to: PAPERCUTZ, 160 Broadway, Suite 700, East Wing, New York, NY 10038
Or call 800-886-1223, 9AM-6PM EST, M-F

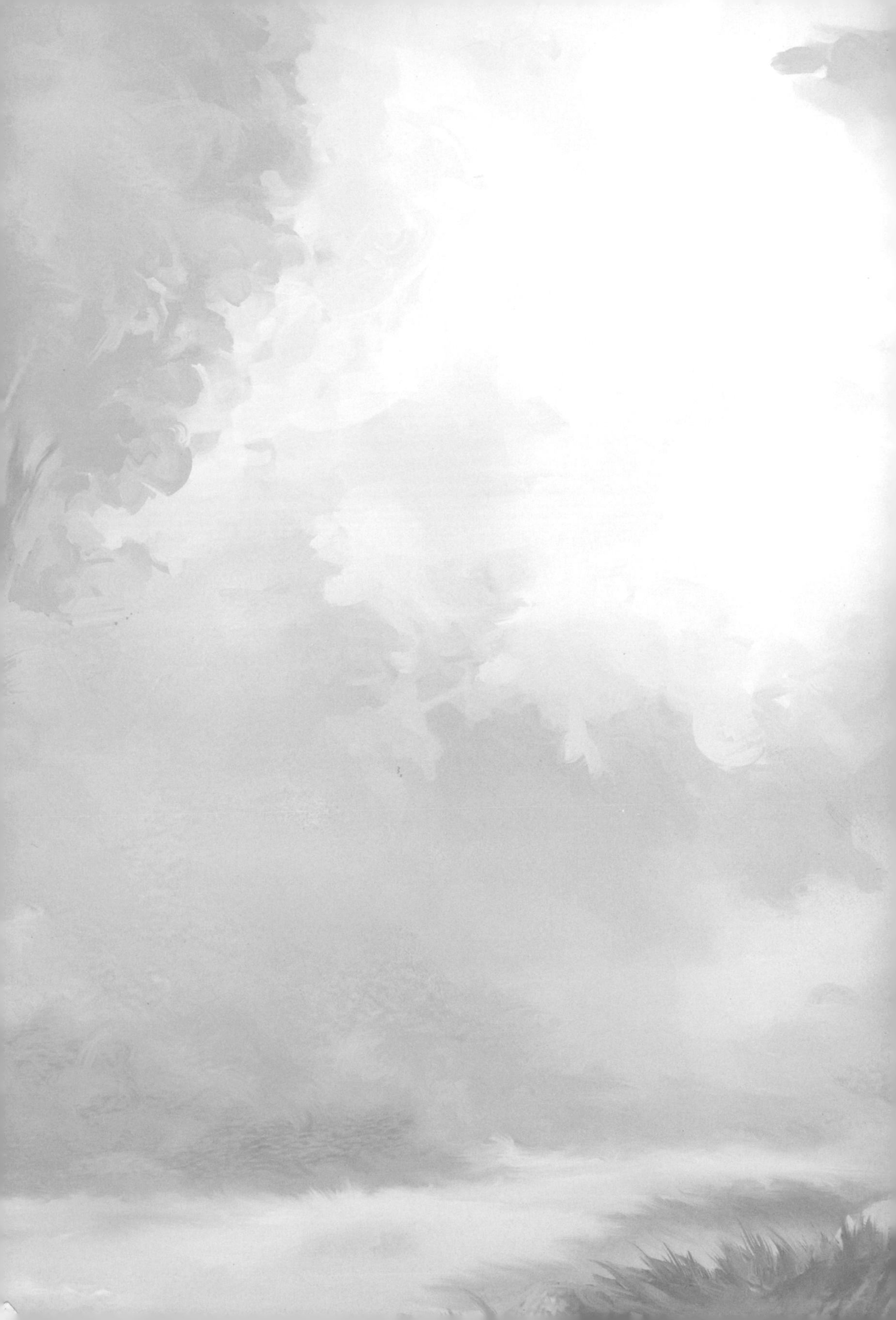